# Scales and Legends

The Merworld Trilogy

Book 3

B. Kristin McMichael

Scales and Legends
Copyright © 2017 by B. Kristin McMichael
www.bkristinmcmichael.com
All rights reserved.

Lexia Press, LLC
P.O. Box 982
Worthington, OH 43085
www.lexiapress.com

ISBN-10: 1-941745-06-7
ISBN-13: 978-1-941745-06-9

Cover design: Jessica Allain
Editors: Kathie Middlemiss of Kat's Eye Editing
Melissa of There For You Editing
Ashton M. Brammer

This book is licensed for your personal use only. No part of this book may be reproduced in any form or by electronic or mechanical means without written permission of the author. All names, characters, and places are fiction and any resemblance to real, living or dead, is entirely coincidental.

# CONTENTS

| | | |
|---|---|---|
| 1 | Chapter One | 1 |
| 2 | Chapter Two | 21 |
| 3 | Chapter Three | 37 |
| 4 | Chapter Four | 54 |
| 5 | Chapter Five | 76 |
| 6 | Chapter Six | 91 |
| 7 | Chapter Seven | 106 |
| 8 | Chapter Eight | 123 |
| 9 | Chapter Nine | 136 |
| 10 | Chapter Ten | 151 |
| | Epilogue | 168 |
| | Acknowledgments | 172 |
| | About the Author | 173 |

# CHAPTER 1

**Standing on the** pier, Sam watched while Whitney moved out of the way and a fish darted past her. She was a bright student and caught on quickly. If she was allowed to join the guard like she wanted, she would have been one of the top people in the group by now. But all she was allowed to do was train. She had a new role to play, just like him, and being part of the guard wasn't it. He was fine with the idea that she would never have to go on patrols. She would learn how to protect herself and not be put in danger when assigned protection duty in the waters around the island. Really, he could live with that, and it was even better that his father suggested it as Sam didn't have to take the blame for holding her back, even if he agreed.

"See? I knew if you explained the trick to that one to her, she'd be fine," Sam's older brother, Nic, said as he watched beside Sam. He was the one officially training Whitney as Sam was busy with his father now.

"I didn't tell her," Sam replied as he watched her move out of the way of the second fish. Just yesterday it would have at least nicked her arm. She'd figured it out herself, and he wasn't about to take credit for it.

Nic returned his gaze to the water also as they continued to watch. Ducking and dodging at just the right time came naturally for the new siren. It had only been a few months since she'd been turned, but she was perfect in the water, a complete natural. He had a feeling her background as a night human might have helped her change progress, but then again it could have just been because she was who she was. Nothing seemed to stop Whitney when she put her mind to it. Whitney had made it through all the obstacles and was already on her way to ding the bell.

"Man, that took you years to figure out, and she did it in one week. Are you sure you're higher up than her?" Nic teased. "I think your mate has you beat."

No one knew that Whitney was a stronger siren than Sam, or the king for that matter. They had kept it a secret, and he made sure she had complete control before she began working with Nic. No one was going to find out where she ranked now. Sam had a feeling his father suspected something after the fight on the island, but she'd played the part of a subordinate since they'd come back to the island and no one could prove otherwise.

Whitney had taken to being a siren like a natural even though she complained about not knowing how to do anything. All it took her was a little practice, and she could do anything Sam taught her. In the two months, they had been on the island full time, she had grown strong enough to be one of the top siren, and everyone knew it even without knowing the real truth of her power.

It was hard to get Whitney to say good-bye to her mainland life, but it was for the best. She still went back to check on her aunt and cousin twice a week, but she was now living on the island full time with Sam. Her family and friends didn't know she was gone the rest of the time, and with Sam's help, they didn't even notice she was gone. She did agree it was better for them since they were all day humans. War was coming, and she needed to be with Sam, her mate. And now he was more set on staying on the island, and so was she. It was the one truly protected place for them, and they needed to stay protected. From all their intel, it looked like most of the mer were slowly siding with the Lara and Undines, and declaring war on the siren.

Whitney poked her head out of the water as the bell rang. She was through the course in record time. Heck, she had probably beat Sam's best. It was like she was magic. She could move as graceful as any mer underwater, but there was power behind her not even the best could match. Sam had a feeling that some of her previous night human was leaking through. She had been a cat for many years, and now a siren. Sam didn't need to worry about her safety. She was a force to be reckoned with.

Whitney waved and blew him a kiss.

*'3:28,'* she told him mentally. Their connection was permanent on the island and easier than ever. *'Two more seconds, and I'll beat your best.'*

*'So who told you how to get past the fish at the middle part?'* Sam already knew the answer, but he had to ask anyway just in case of the very slim possibility someone had told her the trick.

*'No one, silly. I did what you said and thought more about it. It made sense that they couldn't turn as quick as me and that if I got them going to the right with enough speed, I could fake them out,'* Whitney replied, ducking into the water and swimming back over to the pier where Sam waited with Nic.

"Are you going to run her through the land drills again tonight, or is she done?" Sam asked Nic. He wasn't a big fan of any of his family, but now they all treated him differently. With the change in character, Sam now trusted them and had complete faith in Nic to train Whitney to use her siren skills while he was in the water and on land, since Sam hadn't had time to show her yet.

"Again? I'd prefer to not get my butt handed to me by a girl one more time tonight. I've no idea where you found this one, Sam, but you're one lucky guy."

Nic patted the back of Sam's shoulder as he reached down to pull Whitney from the ocean. It was strange to have his brothers be genuinely nice to him, and he still wasn't used to it. It had been weeks now, and they were still treating him better than they had his whole life.

"3:25," Nic told Whitney, who was now standing next to

Sam's brother in a short, pale yellow dress that seemed to make her skin glow more than usual. Whitney appeared confused. "I didn't say go quick enough," Nic explained. "The clock ran three seconds before I gave you the signal. Therefore, your time is actually three seconds quicker."

Grinning, Whitney hugged Nic.

Sam coughed to remind her that she was hugging another siren in front of him. Not that he would ever be really jealous of his brother. Whitney was more than his.

"Don't get jealous, you big oaf," she said, patting Sam's chest. "Everyone knows I'm yours."

That much was true, but it didn't mean he liked to see her hug his brother. Friendly or not, it was still another man she had thrown her arms around.

"So, we are done for today," Nic replied, picking up his dropped timer and making his way off the pier.

"No sparring?" Whitney asked after him as he walked away. She sounded disappointed.

"Not unless you want me as your opponent," Sam replied, catching her in his arms and nuzzling into her neck. She melted into his touch, and that made him want to throw her over his shoulder and march home with her. Whitney laughed as he moved to do just that.

"Sam. I have a dress on," she complained, pulling at the hem with her free hand.

He contemplated if it was worth setting her down or not. She also had underwear on, and he was sure it was quicker to just carry her back to their home. Whitney pounded on his back while she giggled. She wasn't really protesting too much. He had seen her training in the past few months, and she easily could get down if she wanted to. Heck, she'd probably have him in a headlock by now if she were truly angry.

A cough behind him made him stop in his tracks. Sam didn't need to turn around to know his mother was on the end of the pier.

"Samuel, is that any way for the future king to be treating the future queen?" she scolded him.

Sam set Whitney back down, and her cheeks flamed red. She was having just as much fun as he was, and it was rare now that they were allowed to have fun. It was like his mother knew when they were acting their age and appeared to tell them to behave. And since he took his father's offer to be the heir to the siren throne, Sam had to listen to his mother. He thought being king would give him more power to do as he wished, when he wished, but in moments like these, he felt like he had less control over what he desired. Right now all he wanted to do was haul Whitney away and pretend like the mer world wasn't on the brink of war against the siren, with odds that weren't in their favor.

**Whitney snuggled into** Sam's warm arms. Yes, the island was hot and getting hotter as summer approached, but there was something different about the warmth from Sam. It felt good to be roasting in his arms. Maybe because she had thrown the covers off during the night and was chilled from the breeze. Warm or not, it was still air blowing on her. Sam's arms tightened around her as he continued to sleep. Whitney smiled. Even in his sleep, Sam was protecting her. That was just the way he was.

Slowly, she was getting used to life on the island. It had taken a bit of an adjustment when Sam told her she would have to move there, and she might not have talked to him—out loud or mentally—for a few days, but that was behind her now. She accepted that the island was where she was supposed to be. After all, she was a siren, and everything she needed to learn to survive was taught on the island. The siren that went to the shore as teens did it just as a way to learn about day humans. They had to know how to walk amongst day humans without being suspected of being a night human when going for food. Whitney didn't need those lessons. She needed to learn what the siren kids were all taught before they left. Luckily, Sam's mother was the one teaching her or she would have had to be in a classroom with a bunch of preteens.

"Need more sleep," Sam told her. He knew she was awake. How he always knew was beyond Whitney.

"Actually, I feel great and might go for a walk." Whitney sat up now that his arm around her loosened.

"Not without me, and I want to take a dip in the pool first."

Whitney laughed. It was such a day human thing to want to wash up in the morning, but his reasons weren't the same. Sam preferred to let his mer side out first thing in the morning because he claimed it gave him more control throughout the day. She wasn't sure if she agreed, but she was still training every day and spent more than a few hours in the water, so it was never an issue for her. Sam didn't get the chance to be in his night human form often at all now. His father had him working from morning until late at night. What they were doing was beyond her, but Whitney understood his need to swim.

"Fine," she replied, like his dip in the pool was going to interrupt her unmade plans.

"Race you." Sam bounded out of the bed as if he hadn't just been completely asleep and was out the bedroom's patio door before Whitney stood up.

Laughing, Whitney rose and followed him in time to see his blue fin burst out of nowhere as soon as his hands hit the water from his high dive into the pool behind his house. Part of getting used to the island was accepting the incredible place where she was now living. It was a tropical paradise, and practically every house had a pool. Sam's was right outside his bedroom for moments just like the one they were having.

Stepping over to the edge of the pool, Whitney peered down into the blue-looking water. Sam had the interior of his pool painted a deep blue, and beyond his sun-kissed skin, it was hard to make out the rest of him in the water as his tail matched perfectly.

*'The water's great. Aren't you coming in?'* Sam asked mentally.

Sure, she was going to go in, but it was still fun to just stare at him. Even now, after finally getting over the newness of being a mer, Whitney still found Sam enjoyable to stare at. And the best part of all was that he was hers forever. She was pretty sure she was never going to get used to that.

With a graceful step, Whitney plunged into the cool pool water, instantly letting out her night human side. It was wonderful that they didn't have to worry about heated pools in the winter time. Their night human side would keep them warm no matter what, and really the water wasn't too cold because the island was never cold.

Whitney didn't get a minute to look around as Sam came over and wrapped her in his arms. It was the perfect life. Whitney wished it could always stay like this. He grinned at her as he obviously read her mind. Coming back to the surface with their arms still wrapped around each other, Whitney sighed as she caught sight of someone standing just inside the bedroom. Perfect life was going to have to wait, and so was the stroll through town.

"Your father requests your presence." The young mer's voice squeaked as he spoke. Dean was barely old enough to be done with his studies and working on the island. Whitney knew the teen was the favorite to send on running errands for the king because he was the fastest of all the young men working for him, but that didn't make the boy any more confident. He always looked at Sam like he was waiting for him to strike him down for doing something wrong.

"Tell my father I need at least ten more minutes to soak, unless he wants to deal with my siren side not being happy." Sam pulled Whitney back into the water with him.

*'He's not going to be happy,'* Whitney told Sam silently.

*'He's going to have to wait. I haven't been in the water since yesterday morning. The old man has me doing too much, and if he wants me to continue, he's going to have to back off, stop waking me up, and ordering me to his side when I should have time with my mate.'*

Whitney loved his reasoning, but the king didn't like to be kept waiting. Pushing her way back up to the surface, she found Dean still standing there.

"He asked me to make sure you come with Sam," Dean added.

Whitney nodded as she pulled herself up to sit on the edge of the pool, her pink tail flicking in the water at Sam. Dean stared at her unique scales before realizing she was watching him. His face flamed red, and he hurried out of Sam's house, back the way he came.

"Why do they all still act like I'm odd?" Whitney asked Sam as he swam over to her.

"Because you *are* odd. That's what I like best about you." Sam reached up to pull her back into the water.

"Not a chance. I'm going to get a shower in while you soak. I'm not showing up for a second time this week looking like a drowned rat because you won't let me leave the pool with enough time to get a shower in." Whitney pulled back her legs and stood up.

"Only the second time?" Sam raised an eyebrow. It would be more like the fourth time, but Whitney wasn't counting the other two. At least then the king hadn't summoned her, so she could have stayed back to shower and chose not to.

Whitney hurried away before Sam could use his charm to get her back in the water. It wasn't like she wanted to be away from him. The bond made it nearly impossible to drag themselves apart, but she was getting stronger at it. They had to, after all. Sam had a job to do, and she needed to train. It was nice Sam liked to protect her, but Whitney was more than set on protecting herself.

Lathering up the soap and cleaning her hair, Whitney continued to think of how different everything in her life was. The one thing that wasn't different was Sam. He seemed unhappier than Whitney was at being on the island. She could tell he wasn't just missing the long swims in the water that his father kept him from, but he was also missing the shore. She thought it was the singing at his concerts and large crowds that threw themselves at him at first, but she knew now it wasn't his singing career he missed. He missed just being a normal person. On the island, they were anything but *normal* with Sam as the heir to the throne, and Whitney, his prized pink-tailed mate. Normal did sound a bit tempting her though, and Whitney was ready to get a break from this new life. But that break wouldn't come until they dealt with the growing dissent in the merworld around them.

Whitney headed out of the bathroom and back into the bedroom to dress for the day. Sam was still out in the pool soaking. He really needed it, too. He had been growing crankier as the days went by and his time in the water was being cut down to minutes each day. Slipping on a summer dress and flip-flops, she was relieved to have time to dry her hair.

As the warm wind of the blow-dryer blew on her head, Whitney closed her eyes and just listened to the world around her. The sound of the dryer was white noise and did nothing to cover up her night human sense of hearing. Her new senses had developed more as she had been on the island. Now her sight was perfect—she could actually see farther than she knew was possible—and her hearing was even better. She liked to practice picking out certain people on the island and seeing if she could hear them.

It didn't take much to hone in on the king. His voice always boomed when he was excited or agitated, and while she still didn't have a connection to him, she could tell when he was mad or happy. Something made her mind wander to where he was.

"And the second section?" he asked, his voice not yet yelling, but there was anger behind it.

"Closed off. Two of the patrols were attacked, and only four siren made it back. This time it was the Caesg," someone reported to him.

Whitney didn't have every voice on the island down, so she was unsure who it was.

"The Caesg have joined the rebellion now, too?" The king seemed shocked. "First the Lara and Mavkas—I expected that much. Neither one has been happy for centuries. The Undine was a surprise. But the Rusalka, Melusine, and now the Caesg?"

"Father, we knew this was coming. It was one of the predictions we've been working on," a softer voice replied. That had to be Ken. He didn't speak loudly.

Whitney couldn't be completely certain, but he was always the quiet one of Sam's older brothers. While he didn't say much, when he did he made it count. Actually, Whitney saw Ken as the smart brother of the group. He liked to think before acting, which was very out of character for Sam's family.

"Listening in on someone?" Sam asked as he wrapped his arms around Whitney's waist.

She snapped back to the bedroom and shut off the blow-dryer. Her hair was already dry, but she was so interested to know what was going on she hadn't stopped.

"Seems the Caesg have now joined in on blockading the island," Whitney explained. She didn't need to keep anything from Sam. He would be told anyway, and if he really wanted to know, he could always go into her mind.

Sam shrugged as he pulled a shirt on. Whitney was only a little disappointed. The blue lines that shimmered up his torso were hidden from view. He might not have needed his singing career, but she was more than sure there were dozens of girls that longed to see him like this. One more perk of being on the island.

"I expected no less," he replied, not shocked.

Sam was more of an "expect the worst and plan accordingly" type of guy. The old king might have been that way at one time, but now he had a more rose-colored view of the mer world. Sam claimed that came from being on top too long and never leaving the island, but Whitney wasn't sure. His father seemed as sharp as ever, and she had a feeling it had more to do with his son, Tim—Sam's evil older brother—joining the rebellion.

"Apparently, they've blocked off sector two," Whitney explained further. She wasn't completely sure on all the details of protection, but she felt there couldn't be much more left to close off. "So how long before they've completely closed off the island?"

Sam paused as he was slipping into his shoes.

"Not long. If I suspect right, they probably already have the Lobesta moving in to block the last." Reaching down, Sam pulled his shoes on before standing and offering his hand to her. Whitney accepted. They didn't go much of anywhere these days without touching each other.

"Why the Lobesta, and not the Merrow or Selkie?"

They began their walk across the island. Sam had purposely picked a house as far away from his father as possible, but now he had to hike across town every day to get to his new job. Whitney found it funnily ironic, but Sam didn't quite see the humor in it.

"The Selkie will stay out of it until they have no choice."

"But they helped us not even months ago," Whitney interjected.

"Because they owed me a favor. They repaid it, and now they will stay away. Their leader doesn't want to be involved in too much as they like to stay isolated up at the north. In fact, I would be surprised if they even care about what's going on. They like their ice water and hate the tropics, so I don't see them coming back soon."

"And the Merrow?"

Sam nodded to someone who bowed to them as they passed. "The Merrow won't join either side. I'm sure of that. If needed, they will go inland and live in lakes and rivers to avoid it. They don't fight. They didn't in the night human wars, and I know they won't now. Everyone pictures night humans as evil, blood-sucking monsters, but some are nothing like that. The Merrow are nothing like that."

Whitney nodded. She still had much to learn about all the different clans. They had been going over how to tell them apart, which she did think was the most important thing to know, but she didn't know the specifics—like the Merrow loving peace. She never had heard of a kind night human race before. Night humans were supposed to be the monsters of kid's nightmares coming to life, and pretty much every night human she had ever met could be scary if provoked.

Walking across town went quicker than Whitney wanted it to. She had been planning to take a stroll, but the king's plans had canceled that. As they neared, she felt dread in the bottom of her stomach. She didn't know what it was from, but she knew there was something going on. It wasn't until she moved to the island that she started to get feelings about things. She could tell when something good was about to happen, but more often than not these days, she could tell when things were getting worse. It was getting worse. She didn't need to go into the house and see the expression on the king's face. She already knew. Something more had gone wrong during their walk over. Whitney looked to Sam. He could feel what she was feeling, too. He had no explanation as to why she could predict things like she could now, but she was always right.

The siren king turned to Sam and Whitney as they entered. Spaced around his room were Sam's older brothers, Nic, Ken, Lee, Ace, and Ian. All of them except for the missing brother Tim were there. No one smiled as they entered, and the feelings of dread were confirmed.

"What's the problem now?" Sam asked, looking at his father and cutting to the chase.

"They finished their blockade. We're cut off from the rest of the world." The king stared at Sam like there was a silent message passing between them. Whitney tapped into Sam's mind to eavesdrop, as she knew they were doing it to keep her out of the loop. The king had yet to figure out that she could listen in to his son's head, so she made sure to put on a blank face so that no one would notice.

*'And there are seven siren still on land, including the green friend of your mate, Trudy. We don't have a way to protect them, and we can't get them back on the island. They don't stand a chance of surviving.'*

**Whitney didn't have** to keep her new knowledge to herself; Sam immediately turned to his brothers.

"How could you leave anyone on land? We knew this was going to happen eventually. Everyone should have been called back weeks ago," he complained as he turned and scowled at each of them like they were personally responsible.

"We didn't know," Ken said quietly. "This was only one of the possible outcomes we thought might happen, but we didn't know how soon."

Sam turned his glare to Ken, and his brother immediately cast his gaze down. Ken wasn't just quiet; he also avoided fighting, especially with Sam.

"Sam, even you didn't think it would happen this quick," Whitney scolded him. Ken wasn't the one he should be taking his anger out on. It should have been reserved for the king, who refused to call all the siren home. He was the only one responsible for the seven still on land.

Sam seemed to agree with Whitney's thoughts as he turned his anger to his father. "What are we going to do?"

The king shrugged like it wasn't much of a problem. "We

wait it out like we planned. We're fine here for years."

Whitney gave Sam a questioning look. How in the world were they fine? They were night humans that needed day human blood to live, and the siren required more than most. Sam gave Whitney a "we'll talk about it later" look that told her everything. *There must be humans on the island that she didn't know about.* With the population of siren, they must have had a lot of humans. She returned his look with her best, "you better believe we'll talk about it" expression. She was too pissed to attempt to find out more mentally.

"And the trapped siren?" Whitney asked, not giving away that she knew Trudy was there. "What can we do to get them home?"

"They know how to fend for themselves. They will be fine also," the king replied like it didn't really matter. She had a feeling there were no blues, just greens on land, and to him they were disposable.

"And what happens if any of the other mer go on land to hunt them? Will they be fine then?"

Suddenly the men around the room appeared shocked, like that hadn't crossed their minds. The king understood the circumstances, but no one else seemed to. Whitney rolled her eyes. It wasn't just the king who had been on the island too much. It seemed like his sons weren't in touch with reality, either.

Whitney was in shock that the men were clueless. "Don't you guys get that the other mer want to get rid of the siren? They aren't just sitting around the island for sport. They want you dead. Why can't you see that?"

Whitney glanced at the king, but he seemed baffled. His one and only plan was to wait it out, and when the mer clans got bored, they would head back. He really didn't understand that the other mer wanted the siren gone. No matter how many times Sam or Whitney explained, the king thought the clans were just having a little rebellion to get something more from him and would be done soon. He compared them to spoiled children who needed a time out. She turned to each brother, and again got confused expressions. Finally, Nic spoke.

"They can want all they like, but they can't defeat us. That's why the siren have ruled so long. We're the strongest. Even a handful of green siren are stronger than the few fighters they may send after them." Nic didn't seem too worried for the greens, but she could see that he was listening to her words.

"And your older brothers. Were they undefeatable, too?" Whitney knew she was pushing it. They all held a fierce loyalty to their dead brothers.

Sam stepped in front of her as Ace growled.

"What Whitney is saying is that the siren are not infallible. We know it, but don't ever admit it. If Tim has gone to their side, we have to assume he's hatching a plan with them to kill us at least. He won't want any of the royal family left alive. She's right. The siren on land aren't safe, and neither are we here unless we figure out how we plan to fight back."

Sam was always much more elegant with his words, and Whitney was sure glad to have him for that. His brothers seemed to now be listening and considering that it might be possible the others would attack. Even if the king wasn't ready to believe the mer clans meant business, if his sons did, then that was a start.

"But we can sing," the shortest of the brothers—Ian, the one closest in age to Sam—replied, as he was still confused.

"And what if they wear earplugs? Does your song go through that?" Whitney demanded.

Ian shrugged like he didn't know the answer.

"Or how about if they damage their hearing? I wouldn't put it past them to even remove their own eardrums if it meant getting rid of you guys," she continued, pushing. The men in the room needed to wake up. Whitney had seen night human wars between clans before. They hadn't.

Now the men all gaped at her in horror. It must have never occurred to them that someone would damage themselves so badly, but it would make them able to get past the singing. The siren had always been on top. They couldn't imagine a world where that wasn't the way, but they were going to have to open their imaginations a little if everyone was going to make it out alive.

"So how are we going to help those siren on land? It might not seem like much, but when it comes down to hand-to-hand combat, where we will be severely outnumbered, I'd rather have those seven back with us fighting."

And that was all it took to finally make it sink in. The brothers all turned to their father, whose face hadn't changed one bit. He still needed to be convinced. Whitney glanced to Nic. He was currently running the guard around the island.

"Is there no way off the island at all?"

Nic didn't look to his father before answering. "Not if you have a blue or green tail. They are attacking immediately and not asking questions. They don't allow siren in or out, and they just closed off the last two sections we had been using."

"So there might be more siren outside the blockade?" Any more help was going to be useful at this point.

"No. They've killed everyone that got through, and we got the bodies back." Nic was somber about the situation, and Whitney could understand. He was technically responsible for the guard, and he let them patrol knowing what was coming.

"So we need to find a way off the island to get the siren on land, and then find a way back to the island." Whitney was thinking out loud, but she didn't need the guys to respond. She could see by their grim faces that they knew it was an impossible task. Then again, Whitney didn't believe in impossible. Sitting down on one of the couches, she placed her fingers together as she thought. Through the bond, she felt Sam having a silent conversation with someone, probably the king, because whoever it was, they were making him upset.

"I might have one solution," Ken said quietly.

Whitney peered up at the soft-spoken brother.

"No, he doesn't," Sam replied like that ended the conversation.

*'Sam, let him speak. We need to come up with ideas here, and no idea is too out there. Maybe it will lead to a better one.'* She didn't need a reply to know Sam didn't see it that way.

"What did you think we could do?" Whitney asked Ken, and all eyes were on him.

Glancing nervously at Sam, Ken shook his head of dark hair. All of the brothers had dark hair and looked like variations of each other. It was obvious that they all got their looks from their father and little from their various mothers.

"Speak, son. Sam doesn't get to stop every plan, no matter how much he doesn't like it. Whitney is right. We will need every fighting body we have if we want to win the coming war." The king's voice was gentle, as if he knew Ken was scared as it was to talk and any more yelling would make him shut down.

Ken kept his gaze on his father as he spoke. "They won't let anyone through with a blue or green tail, but what about a pink tail?"

"They aren't going to let Whitney through, either. They attacked her on the beach. They know she's my mate," Sam answered in a tone that hinted the conversation was done. "She's an even bigger prize than a blue or green siren."

"But not all of the mer know about her yet," Nic added as he began to think. "We had yet to announce your mating or that your mate is different. This might actually be the way to go. Whitney's been training since she got here, and she's as good as, or better than any of the senior guard members. If we can be sure she gets past the mer around the island, she would be the perfect one to get everyone back home."

Sam glared at the same brother he was just being nice to the day before.

"It doesn't matter if she was announced or not. Tim knows, and I'm sure he shared the details with them. Sam's mate is a blond-haired, pink-tailed mer, but still a siren. Watch out and capture her if you can. She's got a big target on her. We can't send her out. If my loving her doesn't matter to you guys, then how about since we're linked, if she gets hurt or killed, so do I. Is it smart to send her out there?"

Sam was good at swaying people, but Whitney also wasn't about to leave the idea of letting her friend Trudy and the other siren on land be murdered for just being siren. They were teens and completely innocent. She had a very soft spot for the innocent and knew they faced enough persecution for being born to the wrong night humans. They were already pursued by hunters for just being mer, but now they were being hunted by the mer for being siren. It wasn't fair, and she was going to do anything to help them.

"So they will be looking for a blond-haired, pink-tailed siren, but what if they find a brunette, pink-tailed Oceanid instead?" Ken suggested, his plan still growing.

"Oceanids are extinct," Sam replied.

Ken shrugged. "We suspect that, but what if one was in deep slumber and woken by all the mer world turmoil? We were each given our own part of the ocean to live in. Now all the mer are congregating in our part of the seas. What if an Oceanid came back to see what's happening?"

Whitney had no idea what an Oceanid was, but she liked his train of thought. It sounded like a believable story. If she didn't have blond hair, would they know it was her? There were very few mer, outside of the siren, she had ever seen. It was more than likely no one would recognize her, and any forewarning from Tim wouldn't help if she wasn't what they expected to find. Ken was hatching a very interesting plan.

"So tell me more about Oceanids," she said to Ken.

"No," Sam commanded, using his siren power and

grabbing her arm to pull her out of the house.

Whitney would have protested but he was fuming mad, and it was best to let him get off his chest whatever he was thinking. She could always talk to Ken later.

Sam slipped his hand from her arm and into her hand and began walking. She kept pace with him and waited for him to speak. They walked back through town, and she didn't worry about the meeting. Sam was still linked to his father, and they would find out everything.

When they finally got back to their house, Sam went all the way through and back to the water. She knew his short temper tantrum had nothing to do with needing a soak, but she sat down on the edge of the pool anyway. Slipping into the water as a siren, she waited for Sam to join her. He kicked off his shoes and jumped right in, surfacing just inches from where Whitney was. Floating with her head out of the water to feel the sun's rays on her face, she drifted with her eyes closed, but knew he was quite close.

"I can't let you do this. They might figure it out and know that it's you. Then they would have you. I have no idea what Tim would do with you now that he can't have you. I'd do anything to keep you safe. You know that. I'd give away the whole island just to have you. If you want to keep the mer safe, then stay here. Don't put yourself out there."

Whitney flipped around and found herself in his arms as his lips touched hers and they sunk down into the water.

*'I know what you mean, Sam. I'd do anything for you, too, but those siren deserve a chance. They will be killed easily if no one is there to warn and protect them. They're just teens, and they are innocent. If I can go there and help, then I need to try. I wouldn't be able to live with myself if Trudy was killed and I could stop it. You know that.'*

Sam pulled his face back and rested his forehead on hers. He was listening to her words.

*'If you do this, you **will** come back to me. There's no*

*world without you in it. You understand?'*

Whitney didn't smile as she had won the argument. She knew she had him at innocence, as he felt the same way about the mer. Whitney was getting herself into something, and even though she wasn't sure if it was going to work, she had to try. She was right when she said she couldn't live with herself if she didn't try. Trudy was her friend, and Whitney did not believe in giving up on friends, especially when they needed you the most.

*'And you don't go rushing off until we have every detail mapped out with at least three backup plans. Promise me.'*

'*I promise.*

# CHAPTER 2

"Sam, I get it," Whitney said for like the tenth time, annoyance seeping into her voice slightly.

Sam cringed. He knew was starting to drive her nuts, but just the idea of her leaving was hard enough. It was actually time for her to leave, and he was having a *bit* of a hard time with it. Okay. That was a lie. He was having more than a bit. He was having a really hard time with it.

"Sam's just trying to keep you safe, little sister," Nic said as he patted her head.

"Little sister" was Nic's new way to show Sam he wasn't interested in the least in Whitney. It didn't help much right at the moment, but it was a nice gesture from a brother that had been anything but kind to him growing up. Not that it was Nic's fault. They had all been like that before recent events, and Sam was more used to their mean ways.

"With the water tricks I've taught her, I'm sure they won't recognize it's her," Ken added as he stood beside Nic in the tree line, hidden from the water's view.

Recognize her? As a brunette, even Sam would have had trouble recognizing her if he wasn't her mate. She looked like a completely different person with deep brown hair, so much that she didn't recognize herself either. She was no different inside, but Sam had to more than once do a double take with her new 'do.

Whitney smiled as thoughts went across the bond.

"Feels like you're cheating on me, right?" She raised an eyebrow.

Actually, it kind of did.

"Get them to a safe place and then get them back to the transfer island. When we finalize our attack, the protection wall will go down, and you then can join the fight," Nic reiterated Whitney's orders, and in doing so brought both her and Sam back on track.

How little did they really know about her? Whitney wasn't one to follow orders, but good luck getting her to try. Sam wasn't about to correct them on that one.

Whitney smiled at Sam as his thoughts had accidentally drifted across the bond again. She winked at him and gave Nic a serious nod, like she was going to follow his orders. *Fat chance on that.* Whitney still stared at Nic, and Sam's last thought stayed private. Sam was going to have to work on getting back his control as he kept slipping with her. He was letting his feeling leak too much across the bond, but it was hard not to. His mind was preoccupied with worry for her safety.

Nic nodded to Whitney, and Ken did, too, before both of them left. Sam was alone standing just inside the trees. They were on the other side of the island, across from the siren's main city. They'd decided that if she came from the side that the Caesg were now protecting she'd have the best chance. They were one of the newest to join, and the most level-headed. They would likely not attack her first since she looked different, they'd probably question her and allow her to talk to them. All she had to do was play her part perfectly, and she'd be fine. And she had to be fine. Sam was two seconds away from yanking her back to him and running off to lock her in a safe space.

"You can always change your mind," Sam told her as Whitney melted into his arms. He knew he had to let her go, but man was it hard.

"Never," she replied as she buried her face into his chest. There was worry right below the surface, but she would never show that to anyone. Whitney was strong. Always was, and always would be. Sam really liked that part about her.

Resting his chin on her head, Sam took a deep breath.

She always smelled like the tropical flowers on the island. It was going to be torture for him to be around any flower while she was gone, as the reminder was going to drive him nuts. It was unfair that she was the one risking herself to save the siren. That was his job. He was supposed to protect everyone, and he was especially supposed to protect his mate. Now he was doing neither. He would sit on his protected island and wait for her to come home, braving all the danger by herself. Yes, it was completely unfair.

"I'll be back before you know it," Whitney told him, but it didn't ease his worry. "And the guys were right about the hair. No one will know me ... heck, not even Tim will know it is me. I just hope Trudy recognizes me."

"They said it should come out after like fifty washes," Sam replied, gently touching a brown strand of her hair; blond or brown she was still his Whitney, after all. "You can just go home to your aunt's first and wash your hair a zillion times to get back to blond, but I kind of agree that brunette should keep you safer since Tim is still out there."

Sam pulled her tighter. It was killing him to let her go, and yet he had to. He knew it, but he didn't have to like it.

"I'll be back before you know. Then we just have to deal with this whole war crap." Whitney smiled up at him and batted her eyes.

He couldn't help but chuckle. War crap.

With one last kiss, she finally made her way down to the shore, alone. It took every bit of self-control in him to not chase her and pull her back to the safety of the island. With a graceful leap into the water and a flip of her pink tail, Whitney was gone, and he was left to worry.

**First part was** done. She was able to walk away from Sam. It was much harder than Whitney had expected. Their past few weeks together made it almost physically impossible for her to do so. She thought that after the initial "happy to be back together" period the bond wouldn't still be pulling them together, but it wasn't that way. Even now as she swam away, she could feel the draw of Sam. He wasn't in the water, so she couldn't hear his thoughts, but she could feel him, like she was a compass and he was north. She knew where he was. Trying to break free of the thoughts that kept drifting back to Sam, she reminded herself that she needed to focus on her escape from the island.

As she swam into deeper water, she knew there would be mer waiting for her. She was ready to play her part and hoped it wouldn't come down to a fight. Luckily, she was trained for both scenarios, but she'd rather avoid the whole "kill another person" option if possible.

Something came toward her, and she dashed to the side to let it pass. She had to guess it was some sort of weapon as the chain it was attached to was only feet away. A second one came from the other direction, and this time, she used her training to not just dodge, but to go find the person wielding the weapon. Ducking down, she used her water abilities to stir up enough bubbles and dirt from the floor to obscure her so she could get closer. She noticed the brown-spotted tail first and was tempted to drag the mer up to the surface by it, but since there was a second, she needed to use him as a shield. Maneuvering herself behind the first while both of them searched for her in the muddied water, she was able to get behind the Caesg and lock him in her arms. With a push from the water, she bolted them both to the surface. Three more heads popped up at the same time.

"May I ask why you attack an unarmed merperson?" Whitney said to the guys, both looking at her now. The one in her arms was way stronger than her, and it was only by surprise that she was able to get him and hold him in place. Thank goodness for pressure points.

"Siren aren't allowed to leave the island," the guy in her arms replied. He was obviously upset with being held captive. Or it might have been being held captive by a girl.

Whitney didn't know or care either way.

"Then why did you attack me? I'm not a siren. I'm an Oceanid, daughter of Oceanus." Whitney spoke as regally as possible. They had to believe that was who she was.

Suddenly, the fierce faces turned to dismay. The guy in her arms was the only one that couldn't see her or her pink tail.

"Impossible," the guy grunted out.

Now it was time to use a few tricks. Ken had explained that there were a few hot springs around the island in the ocean. She just needed to direct that water to where they were now. She pictured where Ken said they were. Creating a stream, she flowed the water to their location. Keeping her free hand hidden by the bulky mer, she reached down and pulled out the glitter she had with her. Ken was sure glitter, of all things, would be enough. He claimed that all mer like shiny things and little bits of glitter would enhance her trick. As the warm water licked her back, Whitney let go of the glitter and forced the warm water to hold on to it. Swirling it around in the sea in front of her, Whitney drew the symbol that Ken found for her. They were lucky at least one of the siren brothers was big on book learning. He knew the symbol for the Oceanid, and obviously, these other mer did also.

The men across from her dropped their weapons as did the man in her arms. She released him and pushed him toward his fellow mer. His mouth hung open in shock as he viewed her now, also. At least he was over being taken by a girl.

"I've been woken from my slumber by the congregation of non-siren around the siren island. When my father created the mer, he gave each kind their own part of the ocean. Why now do you all encircle the siren? This is their part of the ocean."

The Caesg she had captured seemed to be the leader as they all turned to him.

"We mean no disrespect, great Oceanid. We're here because our king commanded us to be," he replied. "The mer do not want to be ruled, and the siren refuse to let us live as we want to. We're here to end the siren and then return to our homes to live our lives as we wish."

"While that may be, why you are here personally? I'm here to figure this all out and report back to my father. As I see, not all of the mer families are here, so I must talk to the others to get their take on it also. My father wants to be sure to punish the ones that are causing this unbalance in the water that woke me."

The men seemed to agree with everything she was saying. With a nod to them, Whitney ducked back into the water and just swam away, leaving the gaping Caesg in her wake. As she swam, she missed the connection with Sam. She wanted to show him how it worked perfectly. Not a single person followed her. But she knew she was alone now. Sam wasn't going to be allowed to connect with Whitney until she made it to the shore, as their connection could easily be seen by the mer.

While she wanted to swim back to her hometown and just walk out of the ocean in the spot where Sam first took her to be a siren, she knew she couldn't. The other mer seemed to have found his secret spot near shore also, and it was no longer safe. She was going to have to take the long way around, which was good because as much as the men had believed her, she had a couple of them tailing her that she had to get rid of.

Whitney tried not to enjoy her game of hide and seek with the mer, but she couldn't help it; being in the ocean just made her happy. She could have only been happier if Sam was there with her. Whitney ducked and disappeared into the sea grass as she waited to lose her last tailing mer. With her ability to breathe underwater and her control over the water itself, she could easily wait all day. But it wasn't going to take that long. The mer completely missed her, and after ten seconds, she crept back the way she came to find the shore and one of the safe houses that would have a waiting car for her.

After a drive across the state—thank goodness Florida was a peninsula, so it wasn't days of driving—Whitney made it back to her hometown. She hadn't had time to wash the brown out of her hair, but she didn't care. She needed to get to the siren before someone else came for them.

Whitney parked the large van she was driving at the school and went inside. School would still be in session for a couple more hours, and she needed them to leave now. As she walked to the front office, she stopped before opening the door. Her sixth sense told her to wait. Voices within were clear enough for her to make out what they were saying.

"We need to see our niece," a gruff male voice said. "Family emergency." Whitney could feel something was off with the guy. She didn't know who he was, or what he was doing, but it just felt off.

"Let me see here," the kind, older secretary said as she typed away. "Callie happens to be in Phys Ed right now. I will message the teacher, and she will send her right here." That seemed to appease the guys as they sat down with their backs to the frosted office window.

Whitney felt the urgency to get to her friend and knew where to find Trudy. Quickly, she passed the office without being seen and headed toward the classrooms at the school. As she passed the gym, a girl she had never met came out. It took only a second to realize the girl was a siren. She had such a better sense of the siren and mer in general now.

"Callie?" Whitney asked, making the girl pause. "Do you have an uncle here on land?"

The girl did a double take at Whitney like she was confused to why a day human was talking about something like that.

"Shoot, I'm Whitney, just different color hair," Whitney quickly explained. She could see the realization dawn on the girl's face.

"Um, no uncles here. None of my family comes to land ever. I think my parents haven't been here since they were teenagers."

Just as Whitney suspected, it was more than urgent to get the siren out of the school. They already had mer there hunting them. If Whitney had left the island even five minutes later, then the siren in front of her could have already been dead.

"We need to leave now, and we need to get everyone left here at school. The island has been surrounded, and I have a feeling the 'uncle' that's waiting isn't here to take you home."

The shocked girl just stared at Whitney. Whitney rubbed her forehead. She really didn't need this. Grabbing the girl's arm, Whitney hauled her down the hallway to Trudy's classroom. Without waiting, Whitney opened the door to the room, interrupting the teacher as she talked.

"What are you—" the teacher demanded.

"Trudy is coming with me, and no one knows where she went," Whitney ordered the room. Everyone nodded along with the teacher, and Trudy stood up to follow her. Outside the room, Whitney tapped on her friend's face to get her out of her trance. She would have rather snuck her friend out, as her control wasn't complete yet with her siren voice, but they didn't have time.

"Um," Trudy said as she looked at Whitney.

"We need to gather the last siren at school and leave now," Whitney told her, motioning to young siren, Callie. "Someone is here that's looking for you guys, and it isn't safe."

Realization dawned on Trudy as she finally recognized Whitney.

"Man, I've missed you." Trudy threw her arms around Whitney.

Whitney patted her friend's back. "I've missed you, too.

But really, Trudy. The island is surrounded, and only I could leave to get to you guys. No one else can leave there right now," Whitney said, trying to explain and get them to move all at the same time.

"You're serious about being in trouble?" Trudy finally got the not-so-subtle hint.

"Yes. Get everyone to the back door by the computer lab. I have a van that will fit everyone. I'll go get it and meet you." Whitney didn't wait for her friend to agree. She needed to double check that the strange guys weren't walking around the school yet.

Whitney hurried back toward the front office and could see that the men were definitely getting impatient. They were now standing by the desk again, and she could hear the office lady making a phone call. Rushing by the door before they could see her, Whitney ran out to the van she rented since Sam's safe car was not going to fit everyone. Hopping in, she drove it around the building to meet her siren before the guys went looking. She was getting better at hand-to-hand combat, but Whitney found it could be hard to fight someone twice her size due to weight differences alone, and those men were both at least twice her size.

Slamming on the brakes, she threw the car into park and ran to the door. The siren were rushing down the hallway, and she jogged back to the vehicle. Taking it out of park, she waited as all seven siren rushed from the building and crowded into the van. Before the door was shut, she saw what they were running from—two burly men that had to be the fake uncles. She peeled out of the parking lot and only knew one place to go. They would be safe, at least for a little bit.


**Trudy paced around** the decked-out recording studio. Whitney had explained everything to the siren and how they weren't safe going back, or into the water, until they came up with another plan. Their drop-off island was going to be halfway impossible to get to from the water as the enemy mer were all over the place. On her way back to Florida, Whitney didn't just have to lose the mer tailing her, but also avoid the ones roaming everywhere. It was like going to Disney World in the summer, for all the mer that were in the waters around the island.

"So we just stay here?" Trudy asked.

"No, we need to be close to the island to help and at least by the water. I don't know what's safe. My plans were to update Sam at eleven tonight. I need to get going. You guys make yourselves comfortable here and don't let anyone in. I have the key, so I can get in, but no one else does. According to Sam, Tim doesn't know where this place is, and I have to hope so."

"Tim?" one of the younger male siren asked.

"How long have you guys been here on land?" Whitney looked at the young siren guy. Most siren went back home often. That's why there were only seven left for Whitney to pick up.

"I've been here three months," the boy replied. "I was trying to get used to fitting in, and then I got caught up with doing school. It was harder than I thought it would be. I haven't been back in a while."

Whitney nodded. Knowing she only had ten minutes at the most to talk, she quickly gave them all the details of what was going on with Tim. It seemed like some knew that Tim had deserted the siren and others knew about the blockade that was happening, but no one knew that war was coming. They all seemed to think it was just a phase and soon the mer would go back to their homes. The king had done well convincing everyone that it was fine.

"Unfortunately, that isn't the case. They will eventually attack, and we need to be close to the island if we want to help at all. War is coming to the siren island, and I don't plan to sit in the shadows and watch everyone back there die. I need to talk to Sam, and then we will plan what to do next." Whitney finished up as she grabbed the keys. She was going to have to head farther south to contact Sam and keep their location a secret.

"I'll go with you," Trudy suggested.

Whitney motioned for her to follow to the door.

"I need you to stay here. Sam told me that you have combat training. He said it was protocol for all greens to train because most of them ended up in the guard. I'm not sure about the younger ones, but I need you here to keep everyone safe. Those men aren't going to just stop looking. Just in case they find this place, I need you back here."

"But what about you? If they're looking, wouldn't it make the most sense to look by the water?"

"They won't find me in the water. Nic's been training me well." Whitney gave Trudy her best confident smile. She was hoping they wouldn't find her, but by contacting Sam, it was going to be tricky. It was like tying a string right to her, and she would have to be on her best game to remain undetected.

"Fine, but how long do we wait here?" Trudy didn't believe her. Whitney grinned. That was much like her friend. She was always planning two steps ahead.

"Wait here until someone comes for you, me or the men looking for you. I think I can beat them in coming back. I just need to talk to Sam, otherwise who knows what he will do."

Trudy nodded. That much she had to give her. Anyone that knew Sam and Whitney knew they were meant to be together, and Sam would fight anything keeping them apart.

"I'll be back before you know it," Whitney promised before giving Trudy a hug.

"If it had been Amber left here on land, you would have stayed back with Sam, right?" Trudy teased about their siren frenemy. Whitney grinned. While it would be nice to think she could leave behind such a horrible person who had tried to get her killed more than once, Whitney wasn't sure she could leave any siren behind to be murdered by the other mer.

Slipping out the door, Whitney locked the place behind her. She was sure Trudy was double checking it all, too. With one last look around to be sure they would be safe being left behind, Whitney snuck off to the side of the studio and into the garage. Sam kept a spare car there, and it wouldn't catch anyone's eye like the large, white, eight-passenger van did.

Without hesitating, Whitney drove south to the coast where she thought it would be the safest. She wasn't completely familiar with the area, but she didn't need to be. The song of the sea made it clear where to go, and stretching her night human senses kept her safe. She didn't hesitate before diving into the water and going for deeper water to keep hidden. She could have stayed on the beach and just dipped a toe in the water to be able to communicate with Sam, but she would be seen much easier. In the deeper water, she could hide amongst the plants and sandy bottom if needed.

*'If you made me wait any longer...'* Sam scolded.

Whitney couldn't help the smile from forming on her lips. It was comforting to have his voice back in her head.

*'I had to get everyone to your studio. I got to the school just in time. Two men were trying to get a siren out of the school. They're all safe now, but those two thugs didn't like me leaving with them,'* Whitney quickly explained, and sent flashes of pictures to Sam as she talked to him.

*'Come back right now. We don't need to do the plan. It isn't safe.'*

Whitney just shook her head since she couldn't laugh underwater. *'I'm not going back without them. A couple of them are barely old enough to be in high school, let alone left to fend for themselves.'*

Whitney could feel Sam's desperation across the bond.

She didn't blame him in the least for his worry. Those two men were only part of it. She had seen many mer as she left the island, and was more worried for Sam and everyone back on the island than herself. Outside of the war zone, she was free, as long as she didn't need to feed. She hadn't quite mastered that yet, and she was still feeding from Sam.

*'What do you mean you saw more beyond the blockade?'* Sam had been eavesdropping as usual. Whitney replayed the images for him to see.

Anger bubbled across the bond. Sam was finally seeing why she worried just as much as him, and it had nothing to do with keeping the siren on land safe. When they kept saying war was coming, no one had an idea of what it meant; but as soon as the barriers around the island were dropped, there was going to be death, and lots of it.

*'I can't go back to the island near the siren island. The greens will be spotted long before then, and honestly, I don't think they will be much help when the fighting breaks out. Where can I stash them to keep them safe?'*

Sam's mind whirled through places, but he vetoed them as soon as he thought of them. Finally, he stopped on a place Whitney had never seen before. It was a second island that the siren had. According to his memory, it was all set up to be inhabited, but no one had actually moved there since it was their back-up plan in case someone breached the siren island. The siren would be safe, as the island was guarded by similar spells that kept all non-siren out of it. It would be a secure, secluded place for them to stay.

Whitney dashed back up above the plants to be able to swim freely. She needed to see that the island was safe before she'd drag any of the siren back out to the water. They would have to be quick and get to it before anyone noticed them. Following Sam's memories, Whitney made her way back toward the city the siren called home on land. As she neared, she had to veer off course just a little to avoid scouts that were watching the shore. She couldn't be certain, but she suspected at least one of the guys was an "uncle" from the school.

Easily skirting the mer in the ocean, Whitney made her way undetected to the island. At the rate that she kept crossing other mer, she was pretty certain she would have to take the siren one at a time to the island. It was going to take a while, but at the same time, it would be the safest. She was pretty sure taking a group would be very noticeable.

Approaching the island, Whitney could make out the white, sandy beaches dotting the horizon as she approached.

*'There are two entrances to the village homes. There's the one just in front of you, and one directly on the other side,'* Sam explained.

Whitney swam close to where she could feel the siren magic holding the barrier. Again, in less than twenty-four hours, her sixth sense kicked in, and she felt like she shouldn't go any nearer until she was certain it was safe. Sam felt what she was feeling, but he didn't question it. Instead of heading onto the island, Whitney skimmed the barrier as she swam around to the north side of the island, not letting it out of her sight, but not crossing it either.

As she rounded the last corner, she knew why her senses told her not to go closer. Lights lit up the beach, and there were lights visible in at least a few homes close to it. Someone was already living on the island.

*'Impossible,'* Sam told her across the bond even though he saw it, too. *'Only siren can cross the barrier. To be there, they would have to be a siren, and all siren are accounted for now that you got the greens in the school.'*

Whitney watched someone walk out of the beach bungalow and to the second one across the beach.

*'It seems like it **is** a siren,'* she replied to Sam, sending him the image of his deserter brother.

Whitney was getting used to Tim trying to kill her, but she was unsure what to do as she watched him for a change. It seemed like Tim was completely alone and it would have been easy to sneak up on him. With her new training, Whitney was confident she could take him. Heck, her voice alone would be enough to make Tim do as she commanded, but she had the seven greens back at Sam's studio to worry about. It wasn't the time or place to take Tim back to his father.

*'Get out of there. If Tim is using the island, then the other clans know where he is and where the island is. It isn't safe.'*

Whitney completely agreed and was already swimming away under the cover of darkness and the plants swaying on the ground of the ocean. It took longer to get back to where her car was, but she wanted to be sure the greens would be safe. There was probably more than one mer looking for the missing seven siren. They weren't about to let even one survive.

*'I'll talk to my father and brothers and try to come up with something. Meet you back here tomorrow?'* Sam asked.

*'I'll try, but if I'm not here tomorrow, try again the next day at this time. I'm going to have to find somewhere to stash the greens, and I don't think staying around town in a good idea. There's enough cash in the studio to let us get away. I plan to take them inland a little. Hopefully, the mer won't follow us.'*

Sam was disappointed, and so was Whitney, but they both knew it was the best plan for now. Inland was feared by the merpeople in general with their need for water. It was a safe bet she'd find safety on land.

*'Stay safe,'* Sam pleaded as Whitney neared the shore.

Whitney was on her own. There was nothing Sam could do from the island, and she had seven people to protect. She was going to do her best to do so, but she needed to know that Sam was going to not start a war while she was doing just that. She didn't need a verbal agreement as she knew he was going to wait for her.

*'You, too.'*

Love crossed the bond from both of them, mixing with

the worry they felt at being apart.

*'I'll be home in no time. Don't worry about me.'* Whitney tried to lighten the mood, but that was halfway impossible to do. The sirens were surrounded by hundreds of mer and Whitney was running amongst them every time she entered the ocean. Life was crazy complicated, and she was ready for a break. She kind of had a feeling that was never going to happen, especially with the way the mer worked in general, but she could keep hoping that there was a solution to everything. Now if she could just find it, maybe she could get that break she wanted.

## CHAPTER 3

**Sam paced his** father's office. He had been with his father and brothers for over two hours, and still, they hadn't found a solution. What he saw in Whitney's head had him worried, to say the least, but his family just couldn't understand. Or more to the point, they couldn't fathom all the mer being against them. He thought they were coming around, but they seemed to only be humoring Whitney. Sam knew otherwise. Even the greens weren't happy about being kept subordinate to the blue siren on the island. The whole mer world hating them wasn't that large of a step. They were all assuming that there were a few mer outside the magic barrier to keep them in, but in time they were expected to just give up and go away. His father was really planning to just wait it out.

"If she can't make it back, then she's smart to go inland," Ken replied, as if Whitney was making sense. Sam didn't appreciate that plan. It was only so long before someone would follow them. Inland or not, the mer world wanted the siren dead.

"We need to find a way back for her and the greens," Sam told his brothers, who were essentially no help.

"Why again can't she just go to the island like we planned?" Nic asked again.

Sam wanted to pull a Whitney and roll his eyes at his brother, but he didn't. They just didn't understand, and he wasn't finding a way to get through to them. None of them were the least bit concerned about the mer blockade keeping them prisoners on their own island. At times like this, he hated the stubborn streak that they all had from his father. He decided to try again to explain the reality of the situation to them.

"We need to prepare to fight," Sam told them for what felt like the hundredth time. No one wanted to agree. He didn't want to go there, but he knew he had no choice. "Look inside my head, Father, and see what I've seen."

The king raised an eyebrow. Sam hated his father in his head, and that was part of the deal Sam had made in becoming the heir to the throne—his father would stay out of his head. At least the king could get that Sam was serious, even if he didn't believe him.

"Do it," Sam told him before his father could make a big deal out of it. He wasn't going to be okay if his father went searching through his memories, but to show him what Whitney saw was necessary since his words weren't swaying them.

The king looked at Sam and nodded. He closed his eyes and Sam focused on Whitney's swim to shore. He projected those thoughts to the front of his mind as his father entered it. It was always a creepy feeling to have someone else in your head that wasn't your mate. When Whitney entered, it felt like his other half. His father didn't feel like that. He felt like someone spying in his mind and Sam would have to do his best to keep everything he wanted secret locked away for the time being. Sam felt the pushiness of the old man and thought to himself he would be happy when he was king, no longer having to let someone have that kind of power over him.

The king pulled out as Sam rewound and was starting to show him the scene again. Whitney was swimming in the ocean not with just a few mer, but tons of mer were swimming past her every couple minutes. There had to be hundreds of them waiting even miles from the island.

Grimly, the king looked at each of his sons.

"War is coming, and we need to make preparations." His word would be believed as he was the biggest skeptic of them all.

This is exactly what Sam had been saying, but it sounded

much more ominous coming from his father. At least now his brothers finally believed him. Sam felt his father push toward the other six men in the room and knew he was sharing Sam's memories with them. They didn't need convincing to follow their father's order, but this way there would be more urgency. The pressure in the room increased around him as they all received the same images at the same time. Yes, Sam wasn't going to miss any of that once he was king.

**Whitney drove the** huge white van through yet another town. They were far enough inland that she doubted the mer would come upon them by accident, but something inside of her said it still wasn't safe. She didn't know where this new sense was coming from, but it was growing stronger. It was like she could predict if something was going to work or not. A nifty new mer power she figured, but she didn't have time to ask anyone about it. And the seven greens in the car didn't really know what powers the blues possessed generally, let alone a new ability she wasn't comfortable sharing yet.

As the sun set, she knew they needed to get to a hotel soon. Everyone would need water and rest as they had been traveling all day and part of the night before. She wasn't sure where they were beyond somewhere in northern Georgia. Passing a run-down motel, she felt it was the best chance to keep hidden.

"Stay inside the van, and I'll go get us rooms," Whitney told the group as she hopped out with the wad of cash from Sam's studio.

Walking into the dingy lobby, Whitney was disgusted by the smell, but even more so by the stains on the furniture in the waiting area. Not her choice of places, but it was conveniently located on the road they were traveling. And she could tell there was parking behind the building, which would make it easier to hide their oversized and entirely too-obvious van.

"I need two double rooms next to each other, preferably on the other side of the building. We don't want the traffic to keep us up all night," Whitney told the chain-smoking front desk person who seemed more interested in the small TV next to the cash register than in her.

"Mm-hmm, sugar," she said, not turning from her TV, but reaching beside her and grabbing two sets of keys. Whitney couldn't remember staying someplace with actual keys. It was strange, but seemed to go along with the gross and weird hotel. "Rooms 104 and 105."

"And your pool is out of order, right?" Whitney used her siren voice to get the lady to agree. That had been another reason they stopped at the grungy motel—the pool. She doubted anyone staying at the place would be using it, and the fence would keep anyone passing from seeing what they were up to.

"Yes, sweetie, out of order." The lady was almost mumbling as she stood up and grabbed a sign from behind the desk that said "Pool Closed – Out of Order". She placed it right where Whitney was standing, and then sat down to watch her show again.

Whitney counted out the correct amount of cash for the rooms and swapped it for the keys before the lady came back to her senses. She still wasn't used to using her voice on people, and found it strange to do. They were always left in a trance that could last hours. She wondered if it hurt them, and even after assurances by Sam that no one was hurt, it still felt weird.

After getting around the building and settling the others in their rooms, she found the pool and was happy to discover that the front desk lady put an "Out of Order" sign on the door to the pool also.

"I had her close the pool, and we can take turns watching by the door. That should get us enough time to get hydrated before we sleep." Whitney hopped out of the van, and the sirens followed. "Whoever wants to go first can go. I'll keep watch."

Whitney showed the waiting siren into the pool. She had just been in the water before their road trip, so she was doing okay. All seven readily jumped into the water, changing into their green monster forms at the last minute. While the blue siren were half human when they transformed, the green siren kept a more fish-like appearance in their night human form. It took a while for Whitney to get used to it, but since her friends at school had all been greens, once she moved to the island it didn't take her much time.

Whitney watched the pool gate as they swam around. Something still felt off. After more than a half an hour, several of the siren got out of the pool; only the youngest still remained in.

"I can keep watch while you go in," Trudy offered.

"I'll just take a shower in the room," Whitney replied. Something told her that she should keep her eyes open for danger, and that something dangerous was certainly near. "Let's go up to the rooms and get some rest. We'll head farther inland as soon as we get enough sleep."

The expressions on the siren faces around her would have made her laugh in any other circumstance. Siren, and mer for that matter, didn't go inland. It was dangerous for them to not be around water. But that would also make it safe. The only other thing they needed beyond water was blood, and she still wasn't too sure how they were going to do that.

Whitney ushered the siren to the two rooms and found the situation was better than expected when she discovered that the two rooms were connected via a doorway that was unlockable. She remembered once as a child being in a hotel with rooms that connected, but since then she had stayed in all new places that didn't have that feature. It was luck that she chose a place like that now, as it was best to keep them all together.

"I need to check with the front desk. Stay here, and I'll be right back."

Trudy gave Whitney a look that said that while the other greens might be okay with being bossed around, she wasn't. Whitney smiled at her friend and nodded, trying to reassure her that she wasn't just being dominant. Trudy must have caught the small strain that came through her smile because she nodded back.

Shutting the door and hearing it lock behind her made her feel a bit better, but being on the second floor wasn't too reassuring for a quick getaway. She had expected rooms labeled 100 would be on the lower level, but they weren't. Heading down the open staircase at the end of the motel walkway, she slowed as she came to the bottom step. Cautiously, she made her way around the corner. There was a car parked outside the main office that hadn't been there before. Quickly she turned back and went to the van. Luckily, she had grabbed her keys on the way out. As she walked to the van, Trudy came outside the room.

"I'll be right back," she called to her.

Trudy nodded and returned to the room.

Whitney drove the van out the back driveway of the motel and around the corner to a vacant lot. It would be better to not have the van around drawing attention to their stay at all. Why she hadn't thought of that before was beyond her. The small wooded area between the lot and motel was enough to keep it hidden from view, but close enough to run to if needed. Whitney hurried back to the motel and checked for the car. It was gone. Keeping to the shadows, she made it back to the front office.

Inside was the same lady, and she appeared to be still dazed. Whitney hadn't used that much power on her, or at least she hoped not. Whitney stood in front of the older lady and watched as she didn't even notice her there.

"Did my friends just stop by?" Whitney asked.

Her glassed-over eyes gazed back at Whitney. She didn't need to use any force; the woman was still too gone to care.

"I doubt they were your friends. They looked like mafia guys searching for some blond girl with a bunch of high school kids," the lady finally answered.

Whitney nodded and hurried back out of the office. Climbing the stairs two at a time, she went back to the rooms and the waiting siren. Inside, most of the siren were already asleep. No one needed to tell them to sleep, they had gotten the hint that Whitney wasn't going to slow down anytime soon. Whitney walked over to Trudy who was still awake.

"Problem?" Trudy asked, pulling her red curls up into a ponytail.

"Possibly. I think we need help," Whitney replied.

She had thought of every option she could, but this was getting trickier. The farther they went inland, the worse it would get as they would be getting into other night human territories. And there was the blood problem. If they fed on humans in someone else's land, they would be hunted by them, too. So far she was running out of ideas, and all she really knew was that she had to keep those seven siren safe. Siren or not, they were innocent night humans.

"Is there anyone you trust?" Trudy asked. She knew everything about Whitney's former life in the night human world.

"I trust Cassie, but her mate is the beta of my old clan. If I tell her, it's as good as telling him," Whitney replied. She had gone to school with Cassie for several years, and for most of it Cassie's mate, Nate, was a jerk. It was only right before she moved away that Whitney saw that he wasn't always a bad guy. That still didn't make her trust him. He was a legitimate night human. The night human council recognized the skinwalkers as a clan. He would have to turn her over if he knew, whether he was a jerk or not.

"Is it bad enough that we need to take the chance?" Her friend verbalized what Whitney was already pondering herself. Trudy didn't wait for an answer. Instead, she hugged Whitney. "Thanks for coming back for us. We would have never known until they killed us."

Whitney patted her shorter friend's head. She would always come back for friends, and now that she thought about it, a new feeling that felt much like the skinwalker she once had bloomed inside her, too. She would protect the innocent. That part of her was always there, but now as she looked around the room sprawled with sleeping siren, she knew it was a part of her that would never go away.

"Get some sleep," she told her friend. "I guess I have a phone call to make."


**Whitney sat nervously,** gazing out the window. She knew calling her friend in the middle of the night wasn't going to wake her, but she still felt anxious about the whole situation. At least Cassie was still Cassie, and she hadn't asked a single question. Oddly enough, all she requested was a picture of the nearest tree and told her she'd be right there. Whitney had no clue what that meant, but Cassie was a witch, and Whitney had to guess it was some new spell she was using now. Cassie assured her that Nate would be fine with her visiting. Whitney hoped that was true and Cassie's mate would let her come. He was almost as protective as Sam.

As the air around the tree began to shimmer, Whitney realized something was happening, and it was probably best if she got closer to that tree. She left the motel room and locked the door behind her just to be safe. By the time she made it down the steps and to the tree, Cassie was leaning against it with a large, black panther lying only feet away.

"Ah, so that's how Nate lets you leave the house. He sends Jared with you," Whitney teased about the cat.

Cassie threw herself into Whitney's arms, and the panther didn't lift his head. Whitney laughed as Cassie knocked her off-balance, and they both ended up on the ground. It had been a long time since they had last talked, and even longer since they had last seen each other. Now that she was an outlawed night human, Whitney wasn't sure she was ever going to see Cassie again.

"I've been waiting like months for you to call me back," Cassie scolded her as they both sat up.

Whitney shrugged. She had one big excuse for not calling her friend back, and she wasn't happy about having to tell her secret. Of anyone, Cassie deserved a break from the night human world drama. Her friend had endured more in the night human world without even knowing she was part of it for most of the time. Whitney always tried her best to not even talk about the clan Cassie belonged to and just let her have a life without all that. Now there was no getting around it.

"Did you bring the blood?" Whitney asked. She wasn't particularly hungry, but she could tell that a couple of the teens upstairs were.

"Of course." Cassie patted a cooler right beside her. "I've been practicing the whole travel-by-tree thing and can bring non-sidhe with me now. All it took was getting the spell right." That made more sense now. Cassie's father was a sidhe night human and her mother a witch. It didn't surprise Whitney in the least that Cassie found a way to combine sidhe traveling with magic.

The panther beside Cassie lifted his head. Cassie reached over and petted him like he was a family pet and not a two-hundred-pound predator watching over her.

"I know. I'll get to that," she told the black cat. "So Jared is a bit on edge because of your new self that you failed to mention the last time we spoke."

Whitney shook her head. Sam was convinced she wouldn't have to worry about her friend and the skinwalkers finding out she was a night human again, because the siren were so secret that most people had never met one, but it was Cassie. She was smarter than most people. Whitney had a feeling she couldn't fool her friend and asking her to bring blood was kind of a giveaway anyway. And it seemed like the panther wasn't fooled, either.

"Long story short?" Whitney asked. Cassie bobbed her head to say okay. "A few months ago I almost drowned, and my swim instructor happened to be a night human. He thought he was saving me and instead accidentally turned me. Now I'm a siren."

Cassie covered her mouth in shock. She'd obviously been expecting that Whitney was a night human, but she wasn't expecting a siren or that she had been turned accidentally into one. It was a shock to Whitney, too, but at least she had months to come to terms with it.

"Wait a second. You're a mermaid?"

Whitney shrugged. That was as close as any night human was going to think of her. The mer might be hung up on their different clans, but the rest of the night human world wasn't. Siren meant mermaid to them. Actually, Whitney tried to hide her smirk at the thought of calling Sam a mermaid. He would love that one. She would have to tell Cassie not to call him that if they ever met.

"Yep, pink tail and all." That was as much of a description as Whitney had for her. The rest of it had to be seen to understand the whole swirly body marks. The panther let out a grumble. "And don't you even think about eating me. I might have a fish tail, but I don't taste like fish."

"So you need the blood because you're an outlawed night human? Makes so much more sense now," Cassie deducted.

"And you can't tell Nate. He'll tell your uncle, and then the hunters will come again. I have enough to deal with without having to fool hunters."

"Again?"

Whitney shrugged. "It's been a busy few months. Hunters are the least of my troubles right now. I called you because I need help. The mer world is at war, and basically, it's all of the other mer clans against the siren."

"You're a siren, right?"

"Yep. I was lucky enough to join the clan everyone basically wants to kill. It's been a blast. But at least I got Sam. That makes it a bit easier to deal with."

"Sam?" Now Cassie was really interested. The whole time they'd grown up together, neither Cassie nor Whitney had ever had a boyfriend. Cassie's uncle and now the alpha of her clan forbid anyone from dating her, and Whitney wasn't a witch. The skinwalkers all had a witch as a mate. So neither of them had much of a dating life.

Whitney felt a blush coming to her cheeks. *Shoot.* She shouldn't have said anything about Sam. Now she was going to have to admit that she had a mate.

"We can discuss Sam later." She hoped avoidance would work. "Right now my problem is that I have seven siren up in those two rooms, and we're being hunted by other mer. I didn't think they would follow us inland, but they did. The goal of the other mer clans is to completely kill off the siren. I know the night human world couldn't care less what happens to a group of outlawed teenage siren, but I do. They're just teens, and are completely innocent. They had nothing to do with the night human war. They're good kids who've never harmed a human, and they don't deserve to die for simply being born siren. I don't know what else to do. If the mer come back, I don't know if I can take on two fully grown mermen and keep everyone safe. I need help, and that's why I called you." Whitney spat it all out and hoped Cassie was following along.

"Wow, and I thought my life was busy," Cassie joked, trying to ease the stress she could see in Whitney. Whitney gave her a meager smile. "I'll help you. You know I always will no matter if you are an outlawed night human or not. I really have no idea how you could be, but I don't care. You're my best friend and always will be. Besties have to stick together. And besides, you helped me with all this night human stuff before; now it is time for me to pay you back."

Helped her? Whitney did what any friend would do for

their best friend. She made sure that Cassie knew the truth and knew that she was there for her at any time.

"I'm sorry I didn't tell you earlier. I didn't want to get you involved in all of this, and I really didn't want to get the skinwalkers involved. This whole outlawed thing makes it all messy." Whitney was beyond relieved. She had been worried all along that even though they were best friends, Cassie would find her being an outlawed night human a problem.

"Don't worry. I'm not going to tell Nate. I've gotten really good at keeping a barrier between us, so we don't share everything. A girl's gotta have her secrets, after all."

Whitney smiled and laid her head on her friend's shoulder. There was so much stress from just being a siren already, and being chased after was exhausting. Having Cassie there made her finally feel like something would go her way. Cassie was magical, and not just because she was a witch and sidhe combined into one. She had some sort of luck on her side, and Whitney really needed a little of that right now.

"So why were you going inland?"

"The mer like to stay near the ocean. If we go more than twenty-four hours without water, we become dehydrated and dangerous. Most don't want to take the chance, and there's the problem of feeding. If a mer feeds inland and leaves a trail, then other night humans will know about us. This way we stay a secret."

"They do know it is the twenty-first century right? There's running water everywhere."

"I know. I think they know, too, but I can't be completely sure. They're so weird, Cassie. Nothing like the skinwalkers. Some of the mer have been on the island for decades longer than we've been alive. Do you know how much has changed and they don't get it? I think at times they don't want to. They like being isolated, but that doesn't help us now. I have to figure out what to do to keep everyone safe."

"I have an idea, but I need to talk to a few people," Cassie said as she smiled.

Whitney stared at her friend. She thought she was there to help.

"Cas, you can't tell anyone about us. If they knew siren were still alive, I'd never be able to come back to land." That was one of Whitney's biggest worries.

"I'm not going to tell anyone. There's one person I know that will keep it a secret and help us. I promise you can trust him."

"Him? You aren't going to tell Turner? Yes, he's cool, and I doubt he would turn us into the night human council, but I don't want to get him involved. He's a good guy." Whitney had met Turner Winter, a night human werewolf, when they had gone on a road trip a couple years ago. He'd told them if they ever needed any help, he'd be there for them, but that didn't mean Whitney wanted to call him. She wanted to keep anyone she knew and liked out of the mer war that was coming.

"No, I'm not going to tell Turner—unless you want me to. I know you had a crush on him …"

Whitney knew what Cassie wanted, and she wasn't going to admit who Sam was. Not right now. They could talk about boys some other time. Right now she needed to get the seven siren she was protecting somewhere safe.

"Do I know who you are going to talk to?"

"Know of him? Most people do, but I don't think you've ever met him. He's like an uncle to me now, or something." Cassie shrugged, keeping her secret of the mystery guy as much as Whitney was of Sam. "Jared will stay here with you." The panther lifted his head and gave her a hard stare. "He will stay here with you and alert you if any night humans come around. I'm going directly to the village. I'll be safe, and Nate will be fine with that. After I talk to him, I'll be right back."

The panther still stared at her.

Cassie stood up and dusted her hands off on her pants before offering a hand to Whitney. Standing beside her friend, Whitney looked at the large cat that was now pacing a little bit away from them, like he was actually contemplating what Cassie had said.

"Is he really in there?" Whitney whispered. The cat probably heard, but she still felt like she needed to whisper.

Whitney knew who the panther was. He was the reason she was still alive and not dead like her mother, father, and stepfather. When an evil witch tried to take away her night human to make himself stronger, Cassie and her two mates stepped in to help Whitney and her brother. Jared, as a person, died that same night, but the cat he once could turn into was still alive. No one understood why the cat part of him lived, but it did.

"Yes. He's in there. He still hasn't spoken to me, but I know he's there." Cassie turned back to the panther and gave him a sad smile. Jared wasn't just one of her mates; he'd been her best childhood friend for many years. Obviously, Jared was still a sensitive subject.

"Thanks for coming to help me," Whitney told Cassie as she moved back toward the tree she had come from. It was then, as the moon peeked out of the clouds that Whitney saw it—Cassie sparkled. Honest to goodness sparkled. Her skin had a slight translucent quality that glittered in the moonlight.

Cassie shrugged at Whitney's shock.

"It's the bit of night human in me. We still don't know how much or what it means, but yes. Your eyes aren't playing tricks on you."

Whitney nodded, though she had no idea what that meant. No one ever met the sidhe ... well, no one accept for Cassie. But she was part sidhe, so that made sense. What sidhe were like, or what they could do, was a mystery to everyone.

Without saying anything more, Cassie placed her hand on

the tree she had come from and disappeared.

Whitney stared at the tree for a few moments, like she expected something more to happen. It was strange to see her best friend just melt into a tree, but then again, when Whitney finally showed her mer tail, Cassie was bound to think that was strange, too. Life was much simpler when they were together growing up, but now apart they were growing in different directions. At least Cassie was still Cassie, even if she had some new tricks. Whitney hoped she was still herself, too, and maybe she hoped more than a little whoever Cassie was going to talk to would be as understanding about the siren as Cassie had been.

"The rooms are 104 and 105," Whitney told the large panther that was still just watching her. How Cassie knew Jared was still inside was beyond Whitney, but she was going to have to go with that. Otherwise, her friend had left behind a pet that could bite a man, or mer for that matter, in two.

The black cat nodded, like it understood what she was saying. Who knew? Maybe it did.

Whitney picked up the cooler, and began walking away. The cat followed like a well-trained pet. She just shook her head. This was going to be a fun one to explain to her siren companions. Maybe she'd be lucky, and they'd all be asleep, so they wouldn't notice the presence of the silent cat. As Whitney reached the door and unlocked it, the panther stopped to give a low growl. Whitney looked back at him. He was still by the stairwell with a view of the cars coming into the parking lot.

"Night humans?" she whispered, and the cat nodded back. Whitney finished unlocking the door and moved to hide inside. "I'll stay inside with the siren. Do you want to come in, too?"

Whitney turned to see his response, but the panther was instantly beside her, pulling on her shirt with his teeth.

"Okay, not inside. Should I get the siren to come with us,

or is this just a mission for the two of us?" It was difficult holding one-way conversations. It would have been easier if Jared had turned into a talking cat, but she wasn't about to tell him that with his teeth so close.

The panther let go of her shirt and nodded to the siren. Well, okay then, rest time was up. At least they got a swim in, and the cooler she had brought up with her was filled with blood for everyone.

"Everyone up," Whitney said in a loud whisper. "Time to leave and we need to go fast." She wasn't sure how much she could tell them, but the panther was getting impatient with the siren as he waited at the doorway, even if it was less than a minute. The siren had been sleeping, but no one seemed to be in a deep sleep. Going inland had put them all on edge.

Her voice was enough to get everyone up and going, even as they rubbed their eyes, but the sight of the large cat in the doorway made one of the younger female siren in the group look like she was going to faint. Whitney just shook her head. There was no way these siren were going to be any help in a fight. She needed to get them somewhere safe, and it seemed like now was better than later. The panther's tail hit the door, and everyone but Whitney jumped.

"I think that means *leave now*," Whitney told the group, now huddled in the front room behind the black cat in the doorway.

Everyone followed Whitney as they made their way out into the exposed hallway. Turning to go to the stairs, Jared padded quickly in front of the group and shook his beautiful shiny black head. With a nod of his chin, he indicated to go to the opposite stairwell. No one questioned, following the cat as they took off the way he indicated while he stayed behind to guard the tail end of the escaping group. Then again, who in their right mind would tell a large cat that almost could look you in the eye that you wanted to do it different? It seemed like panther Jared was more than in charge of the situation, and Whitney knew for sure she should let him be. He seemed to sense was what going on better than her new growing senses.

Once down the staircase, Whitney made everyone hide against the side of the building. The van was closer to the other staircase, but she trusted Jared, and he said it wasn't safe. There was no way he'd have saved her years ago just to get her killed on purpose now. Luckily the siren seemed to just follow her lead and trust the cat for the most part, too.

"The van is behind those trees," Whitney told the cat. He nodded and began walking away from the building, toward the other end of the woods.

While she didn't mind a stroll in the woods, she wasn't so sure how her siren would take it. They were more water-based animals, but they were going to have to suck it up. Once everyone was inside the trees, the panther paused long enough for Whitney to look back to the motel. There on the second floor were the same two guys that had come to the school to get the siren. How Jared knew they were on the other side of the building was beyond her, but Whitney was grateful that Cassie had left him behind. He'd just saved her from having to try to take on two very large mer.

## CHAPTER 4

**Sam knew before** he touched the water that Whitney wasn't there. He had hoped that he could talk to her even though they still hadn't come up with a plan for her and the seven siren she was protecting. He just wanted to hear her voice and know she was okay. For now, he was going to just have to trust that she was which was hard to do.

"You and I both know she's smart. She'll be fine. There's no way the other clans will take her," Nic said as he sat beside Sam on the dock.

At least that much was true. She had proven to both of them again and again that she knew how to be a siren and, more importantly, how to be a night human. Of anyone, she probably had the best chance of fitting into the night human world inland.

"It doesn't make it any easier," Sam admitted, staring out at the dark water.

Nic laughed. "Are mates supposed to be easy?"

Nic stood up and patted Sam's shoulder. Without Whitney to communicate with and get updates from, Nic left his younger brother sitting on the dock.

Sam stared out over the water, willing Whitney to be able to hear him. *I miss you.* Other types of night humans didn't need water to communicate with their mates. Why couldn't he be one of them? Nothing came back. It was the water that connected them when they were far away, and at times like this one, Sam secretly wished the whole world was covered with water. Okay, he didn't really wish that, but it would make talking with Whitney easier. But it definitely wouldn't make being apart any easier. That, he had a feeling, would never be easy.

"Do you feel the change in the air?" Sam's mother was standing behind him now. Her long, dark hair hung past her waist and blew in the slight night breeze.

"Change?"

War was hanging over the siren, and that was one big change. Sam wasn't sure he was ready for the war that was going to happen. He had a feeling that if the mer were eager to attack, that meant they had figured out a way to get around the power of the siren voice. Sure, if they strictly fought underwater the siren couldn't control them, but the siren were smart enough to not do that. They knew their power was solidified on the surface where sound could be heard better. War was coming, and the siren weren't ready for it.

"You brought magic back to the mer world when you made your mate. Your father doesn't want to admit it, but I will. I might be over twenty years younger than him, but I'm not as young as all of you are. I've seen the magic that makes mer tick. I've felt the ocean as it brings peace back to our kind. They might have been legends to you guys as kids, but most legends are based on some fact."

Sam looked up at his mother. She was standing beside him now, yet her focus was on the horizon. Beautiful pinks and oranges would be filling the sky in hours, but for now, there was darkness. Sam wondered what she saw when she looked over the darkened water. He also wondered what she was talking about.

"Siren aren't made. There's no way to turn someone into a mer of any kind that we know of. Whitney is special, and not just because she was able to win your heart. She's an impossible wish for you. When looking for answers about the coming fight, you need to realize what that means first."

Sam's mother placed one hand on his head before bending down and kissing his forehead like she used to when he was a child. He turned to look up at her, and she smiled. She was never one to give him answers, but he knew she was trying to lead him to a solution. Sam's mother had never been accepted by the siren to be queen, as some still whispered that she wasn't really a siren. He had seen her blue tail with his own eyes, so he didn't doubt they were lying, but as a child, he never understood why they thought that. Now as an adult, he better saw how much his mother didn't fit in with the siren. There was something different with her. Now he just needed to figure out what she wanted him to see.

**Whitney stood by** herself in the middle of a lush garden. She could hear the water of a fountain tinkling in the distance and voices of people all over as they went about their daily lives. The sun was just beginning to come up, and a lot of the residents in the grand building before her were going to sleep for the day. They were called night humans for a reason. Many night humans couldn't stand the sun and lived only at night time. And there were night humans all over the place. She couldn't help her heartbeat picking up.

Wishing Cassie had come with her, she tried to calm down. Cassie had to stay behind because Whitney didn't want the other seven siren involved. Cassie and Jared would keep them safe until she returned for them, if she came back at all. The night human council that had declared the siren enemies was not something to take lightly, and it was very possible they wouldn't even let her defend herself. Her chance of leaving alive was slim, but it was the best option they could come up with.

A man in a black suit with a crisp white shirt walked down the garden pathway. When he got close enough, Whitney was ready to curse under her breath. Cassie had involved Turner after all.

Turner grinned as he reached her and swooped her into a hug.

"So how has my long, lost sister's bestie been? Last time

I saw Cassie she was complaining that you had dropped off the face of the earth."

Whitney just smiled and shook her head as he set her back down. After the weekend spent with him in his hometown, Turner was convinced Cassie had to be related to him since they had the same sense of bad luck in love. Actually, Cassie would have loved to have an older brother, and Turner would have been an awesome one if he'd had any younger siblings. They were more than kind of perfect together as siblings should have been.

"I told her not to get you involved," Whitney finally added.

"Involved? She wanted you to go before the night human council, which means I'm automatically involved."

Whitney scrunched up her face in confusion. That made no sense whatsoever. Turner wasn't on the night human council. He wasn't even a lead for a night human race. His father was the ruler of the werewolf-like clan called the lycan, but Turner was the younger son and not set to inherit his father's post. Only leaders or their children could be on the council, so that meant there was no way he was.

Turner didn't explain as he looped his arm in Whitney's and pulled her back toward the massive building she had been staring at before.

"I like having people around that don't melt in the sun. You can't believe how boring it gets around here when the sun comes up." Turner led the way into the building. People continued on their paths without acknowledging them.

While Cassie seemed to know right away that Whitney was a night human—that was probably due to Jared—no one around them seemed to stop on their way as they passed. Whitney was led to believe, as an outlawed night human, anyone that she met would want to kill her. But Sam was more than right, in that it looked like no one had ever come across a siren before. Now she was beginning to doubt her decision to agree with Cassie and to come before the council.

When Cassie came back to them, she explained that she had talked it over with her contact, and the best solution was for Whitney to go before the night human council and ask to be reinstated to the night human world. That would not only make it easy for the siren to access blood, but it also meant that all the other mer would be attacking a legitimate night human clan. Maybe that way they could get a little help in their war. Whitney agreed, as it was the best solution she'd heard yet, but now she was regretting not talking it over with Sam first. She was potentially putting them all in danger.

"So Cas didn't say much beyond the fact that you needed to talk to the council." Turner kept talking as they walked down the hallway toward wherever they were going. For not being on the council, he seemed to know his way around.

"I still don't get why you're here. You aren't on the council." Now Whitney wasn't sure, but she was almost positive that there was no way for him to be on the council. If he was, then maybe her job would be easier. Turner seemed to like her enough.

Turner gave her one of his million-dollar smiles, slight dimple and all. "Oh, I'm not officially on the council, but since I'm a keeper to the head of the council, I basically know everything going on. It's like being on the council without having to do all the boring stuff."

"Wait a second." Whitney stopped them in the hallway. "You are notoriously single. When the heck did this happen?"

A keeper in the night human world was like one step away from being a mate. Some people, not Sam and Whitney, took things a bit slower.

"I'm still single. That much hasn't change. Arianna has five keepers, and one of them is her mate already. I'm just kept around as a souvenir blood bag." He grinned as he spoke and then began laughing.

Whitney wasn't sure what was funny. Why would charismatic, handsome, night human Turner Winter be the keeper to someone that was taken? And why the heck was it funny?

"She heard me say that once and hates it when I describe it that way," Turner explained. "The truth is, Arianna is a really good friend of mine, and I stick around because I want to. She doesn't make me stay, and sometimes I think her mate would like me to leave, which is more than enough reason to stay."

"So you're not part of the council?" Whitney tried not to sound disappointed, but her chances were much better with him on her side.

"Hey, don't sweat it. I got your back, and since I have a direct link to Arianna, I can make sure she sees the truth. And trust me, Ari is a good person. She would never let something bad happen to someone like you."

Whitney nodded as they began walking again. It wasn't telling the truth that was the problem. It was more like history was the problem, and there was nothing anyone, including Turner, could do to change history. All she could hope was that the council could see that she wasn't part of that history, just like the mer on the island. Very few there were even alive for the mer wars, and those that were, were now old and senile anyways.

"You're lucky Devin told the council to stay longer. Otherwise, they wouldn't meet for another week," Turner said.

Lucky? Maybe, but she still felt a little lost. Cassie never mentioned who she was going to see, but it made a lot more sense now. Devin was the sidhe king and a very good planner. Cassie had explained to her once how he became the king of the sidhe night human clan without actually being a night human. That had to be more than luck.

Whitney was now wishing no one had told them to stay. Maybe it would be better to come up with another plan. She didn't need to let everyone know that siren were still out there. For all they knew the siren were dead or there were very few left. If no one in the large house even recognized her, then their chances in the night human world would be good. She could go on hiding with the seven siren she was protecting and wait it out. There had to be another option. Whitney was regretting her decision to say yes to Cassie's plan.

They had just arrived at a cracked open door. "Bring her in," a soft female voice said from inside. And it was now too late to go back. Whitney was stuck.

Turner pushed the door and held it open for Whitney to pass through. Her feet felt like they were trudging through syrup as she tried to walk forward without falling face first in front of five of the strongest night humans around. Turner motioned to a seat in the middle of the group, and Whitney put on her best brave face as she walked in and pretended like she wasn't scared to death of what she was doing. Bolting seemed like the best option, but it was too late for that and Cassie had dropped her off through a tree. Hence, she didn't technically know where she was.

"Welcome," the same soft voice said directly across the table from her.

The petite blonde was sitting in a chair where her feet didn't quite reach the ground. Behind her stood a rather nerdy-looking guy with short black hair and glasses, and a rocker guy with long curly hair. Rocker guy looked the scariest as he stood with his arms crossed, showing off impressive biceps and an even more impressive glare. It was better to look at the girl. She, at least, seemed welcoming.

"I am Arianna Grace, the leader of the night human council. Devin told me it was urgent we speak to you, but gave us nothing more than that. He said you would explain why you needed to see us."

Whitney licked her lips. It was now or never. Change was either coming, or she wouldn't be around to have to worry about it. All she wished was one last chance to talk to Sam. If she made it out of this meeting still alive, she was going to never miss connecting with him again.

Arianna, the council leader, smiled as Turner walked around the table to stand behind her with the other two men. Whitney focused on his face for a moment as the only friendly face in the room. Turner didn't do a stare down like the other two, but Whitney was sure she needed to speak to Arianna. She didn't look at the other four people, two sitting on either side of the blonde girl. She had a very good feeling it all came down to the girl in front of her, the leader of the night humans, the girl that couldn't be much older than herself. Taking one last deep breath and tucking her nerves away, she knew what she needed to do.

"My name is Whitney Mallory. I used to be a skinwalker, but almost two years ago a witch used me in a spell, and it took away my night human half." There were a couple gasps, but Whitney kept her eyes on the girl. She didn't smile, but didn't frown either. So far, so good. "A couple months ago while I was taking swimming lessons, I almost drowned. To save my life my swim teacher gave me some of his night human blood."

The older gray-haired lady that had gasped at the mention of losing one's night human was now nodding like it was a logical thing to do.

"My swim instructor didn't know that his blood could turn someone into a night human," Whitney continued, and before the older lady who seemed to like interjecting could make a comment, she spoke again. "For his type of night human, no one had ever been made into one. Using their blood to save a day human was forbidden. To his surprise and mine, I became a night human again."

"Do you wish to press charges and bring this night human to justice?" the older lady asked.

"No. I came here today to get my new night human clan pardoned."

Whitney finally looked around the room. There was the old lady who wore an expression of confusion. Next to her was an older man, who was younger than the lady, but at least a couple decades older than Whitney. On the other side was a large man that barely fit in his chair. He reminded Whitney of how large Turner's father was. Next to him was a tan-skinned young man that could only be in his twenties. It was a diverse group, and she had no way to gauge what they thought of her asking for a pardon.

"Pardoned?" the large man asked in a booming voice that fit perfectly with his outward appearance.

"She was turned into a forbidden night human," Arianna clarified, as if she already knew that Whitney was a siren. Maybe she had come across one before.

Now the animated older lady had an expression of horror on her face.

"A forbidden night human?" she squeaked out.

"I was turned into a mer, specifically a siren."

Immediately, fear laced the faces of the people sitting around the blond-haired girl. Even her two bodyguards, aside from Turner, seemed a little apprehensive.

"I'm here on behalf of the siren. Almost all the siren alive, and mer for that matter, were not alive during the night human wars. They had nothing to do with what happened. On top of that, the siren king forbade his subjects to go on land and kill day humans. They behave just like the rest of the night human world, yet they live in fear each day of being discovered and hunted down for being just what they are. I didn't chose to become a siren, and the guy who made me never intended for it to happen, but now I find myself as part of this persecuted group. That's why I'm here now to ask for a pardon for the siren, and for them to be allowed to live their lives out in the open just like any other night human."

Looks of shock remained on their faces, though no one replied. Finally, the older lady turned to the blond-haired girl.

"Is what she said even possible? Can you really lose your

night human?"

Arianna nodded to her. "Devin examined everything after it happened, and yes, her skinwalker night human was taken from her. The process can kill you, but someone saved her and sacrificed themselves instead."

That was news to Whitney. While Cassie seemed to have a relationship with Devin, Whitney had yet to ever meet the guy.

The lady was finally at a loss for words.

"Can she prove to us that she's really a siren?" the younger brown-skinned man questioned from the other side.

Whitney didn't hesitate and transformed into her siren form. She had been without water long enough now to be a little itchy, but it didn't hurt to change ... yet. The young man who asked stood up and walked around the table like she was mesmerizing to him. She hadn't spoken, so she knew she wasn't accidentally using her vocal night human power.

"May I?" He reached to touch the lines on her arms.

"Look, she's already put Loan in a trance. Siren can't be trusted. I might not have been around for the last wars, but I know that much," the gray-haired man beside the old lady added.

The man called Loan stopped reaching for her and glared at the old man. "I'm not caught in her spell. Do you know nothing about the forbidden night humans? Siren need to sing to do that. I just wanted to see if the legends are true. My people tell stories about the merfolk, and sorry if you have a preconceived notion as to how they are, but I have some idea as well."

Whitney looked up at him. He was much stronger than he seemed to be as he came near her. She could feel the power behind him pulsating off of him, but he didn't try to touch her again. This was someone she was going to need to speak more to. If he knew stories of the mer, then maybe he knew how to defeat the other clans.

"Do you having anything more to add?" Arianna asked Whitney.

She shook her head. There was nothing more to plead. She had explained how she came to be and asked what she needed to ask.

"What about using your blood?" the giant of a man next to Arianna questioned. "Maybe she's only a siren temporarily. One drop of your blood and she might go back to being what she was before. Then we don't need to decide on this."

Whitney turned to Arianna in confusion. She had no clue what it meant that he would suggest she take the blood of the girl who was certainly in charge of the group.

Arianna shrugged. "My blood has been used to find out what true night human someone should be. By drinking my blood, your true night human form will emerge." The blonde wasn't too concerned, but since the hulking guy next to her seemed to think it was necessary, Whitney had to consider it. It was a council, after all, and not simply whatever Arianna decided.

"Will it change me back into a skinwalker?" Whitney hadn't considered the possibility. Once her cougar was gone, she had grieved and moved on. Now she wasn't sure she wanted her cat back. Where would that leave her with Sam?

"It might. What we have found is most people actually end up with a mixture of traits. One of my friends was a dearg-dul that grew wings because there was tengu in his blood. Things like that. I've never seen it change anyone to one form if they were another."

That was at least a little consoling. Whitney wasn't sure she could just leave the mer world behind, or Sam for that matter. It was growing harder each day to not be around him, and there was a great possibility she was never going back to him. But the expressions on the faces of the council told her they weren't about to give her a favorable verdict without trying the blood. It made sense. If she wasn't a siren any longer then they didn't have to debate the pardon Whitney asked for.

The longer, dark-haired bodyguard walked around the table and handed a thin tube to Whitney. She looked at it and knew what it was. She could see the faint red color through the semi-opaque sides.

"So I just swallow this and magic will happen?" Whitney glanced up at the guy handing it to her.

"Something like that," he replied, his voice much kinder than she expected.

Without thinking further, Whitney tossed the vial into her mouth and crunched down, releasing the sweet drop of blood into her mouth. She swallowed it and sat, waiting to feel something. Nothing felt different. Faces stared back at her. They seemed to be expecting a change, also. Time seemed to take forever while everyone stared at her.

"Umm." Whitney had no clue what it meant.

"Try transforming," Arianna suggested.

Whitney changed and watched as her pink tail now glowed in the dim light of the room. That was new, but the tail wasn't. She was still a siren and still outlawed. She could hear the disappointment from some of the council, but she refused to look at them. She wasn't trying to make their lives hard, but it was true. The siren were not the bad guys. Not anymore. They didn't even kill humans now. And she was pretty certain several of the legal night humans still killed humans, but the council didn't prosecute them.

The young man that had tried to touch her before stood up.

"I'll take her outside of the room for your discussion," he told the group, waving to the bodyguard that was now moving forward to stop him. The long-haired guy raised an eyebrow at the council member, and then ignored him as he followed right behind Whitney.

"We have a waiting room right next door," the darker-skinned man told her as he offered her his arm like a gentleman.

"Don't you need to stay here to discuss it?" Whitney asked, not sure why he was walking her out of the room.

"Nah. Arianna already has my opinion on the matter." He opened a side door and held it for Whitney to walk through first. For being young, he had impeccable manners.

"But no one said a thing." The room had been mostly silent, except for the older lady. Whitney had a feeling that they were all ready to say no, but there was no talking going on at all. How could Arianna know what the man thought?

"That's the best, and probably the worst, part of working with a legend like Arianna. She can read minds, so basically any thought I have she knows. Good and bad."

He winked at her as the long-haired guy followed and locked the door behind them. Whitney wasn't sure if he was locking them out of the meeting room or in the waiting room. Either way, it was ominous.

**Whitney sat, but** not patiently. It seemed like the room beyond the door was silent, even though she knew they were debating about what to do. Either the room they were in was soundproof, or they were all talking in their heads.

"I'm Loan, by the way," the councilman who escorted her out introduced himself. "And that brute is Andrew. He's Ari's mate. So please excuse his behavior."

That explained the brooding looks when she said she was a siren. She was finding maybe all mates had the same overprotectiveness that Sam had. Andrew didn't respond, though; he just analyzed Whitney as she sat beside Loan.

"Don't mind him. He's the silent type," Loan kidded, but she had a feeling it was more correct than not.

"Do you think they will let the siren have a pardon?" Whitney voiced what she was really worried about. If they didn't, then it was likely she would be kept as prisoner, if not immediately executed. She would never have a chance to tell Sam that she loved him one last time.

She blew her hair out of her face as she thought of the crap she was stepping in just to save a bunch of people that she wasn't even technically a part of. She was still an outsider with her pink tail, and now the excessive glow made it worse. How was she ever going to hide in the water with a tail like that? Suddenly, she noticed the strand of hair that kept escaping into her face was bright blond, maybe even lighter than it had been before she dyed it.

"Really?" Whitney couldn't help but complain. "When she said the blood would make me into my true self, I didn't think hair color mattered that much. Man, I was just getting used to being a brunette and haven't had to deal with even one blond joke since I returned to land. Great. Now if they decide to let me go, I might die from hearing too many blond jokes."

Loan laughed, and even the brooding Andrew smiled.

"So, what's it like?" Loan asked. "I've heard stories, but they never compare to someone living it."

"Being a blond?" Whitney teased. That just made Loan smile more.

"Being a mer."

Whitney shrugged. How was the best way to describe being a mer? Obviously, Loan was a night human, but he wasn't a mer.

"When I first turned, I thought I was going to be a fish. The skinwalkers all turn into an animal on the full moon, so I thought it was like that. I was worried I would be tiny and go down the shower drain, or get stuck. Being only part fish is a bit strange. And water. That's weirder. I never knew water could sing."

Loan's eyes lit up as she spoke.

"You spoke of legends about the mer. How do you know about them?" she asked.

Loan grinned, showing off perfect dimples in his

caramel-colored cheeks. "My great grandmother was the one who raised me. She used to tell us tales of all the old night humans that were around before the night human war. She had some pretty cool ones about merfolk. She could describe all these different kinds. Some had red hair, others green or orange. And their tails ranged from deep blue like the sea to bright yellow like the sun. Some looked like animals in the sea, with spots on their tails or a thin layer or fur. She described the mer as a rainbow species that came in every color, shape, and size, but the prize was the pink-finned mer that only came around once every two hundred years. She used to claim if you could touch the marks on a pink-finned merfolk, you would have good luck for the following year."

Loan's cheeks reddened at his last admission. Whitney grinned at his embarrassment. She doubted she brought good luck to anyone, but she wasn't about to spoil that for him. His love for the mer was more than evident, and if the council decided against her, she knew she'd found an ally in Loan. He'd make sure she at least didn't suffer.

As she sat next to him, she transformed. Her sudden tail caught his eye as he was looking at the floor, and he appeared stunned to see her as a siren again.

"Go ahead and get your good luck," she told him, holding out an arm that had a purple swirl going down to her wrist.

"I shouldn't," Loan said, holding himself back.

"Well, if it brings luck, then go ahead and have it. I haven't had any since I've been turned into this. It's been just one thing after another. Heck, here I am trying to save the siren, and if they get a pardon, by the time I get back they might not even exist anymore."

Loan reached forward and gently touched the purple swirl. It almost seemed like it moved to be closer to his hand before it pulled back up her arm. She didn't comment on how strange that was, but she had a feeling things might be slightly different because of the blood she drank. Heck, her hair was instantly returned to blond. If her real self was supposed to be a blond-haired, pink-tailed mer, then the blood worked perfectly. Even if she had no clue what it meant.

"Would you mind if I took a drop of your blood?" Andrew asked. Again, his soft musical voice wasn't expected. "We've been trying to collect blood from every night human out there."

Whitney shrugged. What difference did it make now? It wasn't like she didn't just spill the secret of the merworld to the whole night human council.

"At least something good can come from me being here," she added, holding out her arm to him.

"I just need a finger prick," he explained as he came closer without her seeing him actually move. Without a warning, her finger was pricked, and he was sitting back down.

"He's a baku," Loan explained. "A night demon that feeds on emotions and dreams. You don't hear him coming or leaving. Silent stalker, but ugly as sin when he transforms."

"Then I must be fueling him well," Whitney replied, finally tucking that lose strand of hair behind her ear. "I think in the past fifteen minutes I've felt every emotion out there."

This time Andrew didn't smile, but chuckled. Whitney wasn't sure it was funny, but because he was laughing it probably meant he did feel it.

"They're almost ready for us," Andrew informed Loan and Whitney.

Taking a deep breath, Whitney nodded. In five minutes they had decided her fate. It couldn't be good as she saw how they all looked when she told them she was a siren.

Loan offered her his arm to help her stand and walk back into the room.

"No matter the outcome, let me just say you are the bravest night human I've ever met. If you didn't already have a mate, I'd have asked you out."

Now it was Whitney's turn to blush. That just made Loan smile more. She couldn't deny that if she didn't have Sam, she would've easily said yes to that. He was different than all the guys she had ever known. What teenage guy opened doors and offered a girl an arm to help her stand? It was a bit old-fashioned, but intriguing.

The door to the room creaked open, and Whitney's heart picked up its beat. She wasn't sure she was going to survive this ordeal as the suspense alone was going to give her a heart attack. She very well might be only moments away from dying, and getting her legs to move on command was going to be hard. As she pondered her life ending, there was only one thought that kept jumping into her mind. She kept the image of Sam's face in her mind, his chocolate brown eyes and perfect smile. Every little detail down to the wrinkles around the corners of his eyes, to the faint mole he had on his left cheek. If she was going down, she would do it with him beside her in her mind. She really regretted not telling him about it all, and with the bond, if she died, he would die, too.

Whitney sat back down in her seat in the middle of the room, and Loan and Andrew moved to their spots near Arianna.

"We've debated enough and come to a decision," Arianna began.

Whitney looked at her, but focused on the image of Sam in her mind instead.

"We will pardon the siren, as you have explained that they are innocent, and beyond that you are completely innocent as they aren't your clan by birth. In order to tell the siren from the other mer clans, we will need to find a way to differentiate them before we can officially pardon them."

Whitney stared in shock and didn't respond like she should have. She wasn't sure she heard correctly. Arianna just told her news she wasn't expecting in the least. Loan winked at her and brought her back to reality.

"Siren have blue or green fins," Whitney replied. It was easy enough to tell them apart in the water.

"Yet you do not," the old lady added her two cents, as it seemed she always needed to.

Arianna nodded as she stood. Whitney froze in her seat. She knew only a little about Arianna, but she was pretty sure the rumors were that she was the strongest night human out there. Whitney wasn't about to let the girl's small frame fool her. Night human strength had nothing to do with brawn.

*'I honestly don't know if I'm the strongest. There's not really a competition for that sort of thing,'* Arianna's voice rang in Whitney's head. *'And the guys like to exaggerate to keep me safe.'*

*'So you* can *read my mind?'* Whitney replied. Andrew and Loan were telling the truth. Here Whitney thought she could only read their minds and it seemed like she could read everyone's mind. Now she worried what she might have accidentally sent to Arianna.

*'Beyond your cute mate, there was nothing more I saw. That was only because you were thinking so strongly about him. I do my best to stay out of people's minds if I can.'*

Arianna walked past Andrew, and he followed two steps behind. She turned to him and placed a hand on his chest to stop him from coming around the table with her. He stopped in his tracks and gave her a hard stare. She didn't even wither under the pressure he was exuding.

*'I want to try using one of my abilities on you. I think it might help us,'* Arianna explained as she continued around to where Whitney was seated, and Andrew stayed in his place.

*'Um, okay?'* Whitney replied as she realized that Arianna was waiting for an answer.

Arianna gently placed her hands on both sides of Whitney's face. A strange sensation came over Whitney as Arianna's hands warmed up. Whitney watched Arianna as she stood there with her eyes moving inside her closed lids.

She was doing something, but Whitney had no idea what. After what seemed like only a few moments, Arianna let go.

"Turns outs you are right, Cleo, in doubting her being a siren. We have given the pardon to the siren, but you, Whitney, don't need one. You are something that has not existed for a long time, and are not an outlawed night human at all."

Whitney was now more confused than ever. Arianna saw the confusion and continued.

"I know the siren told you about Oceanids as a way for you to get off the island. To the siren who are alive now, and probably the rest of the night human world in general, Oceanids are a legend; they aren't real. What your pink tail proves is that they *are* real. I know that you still carry the spirit of the skinwalker inside of you and want to protect the innocent. I think fate decided that this is a way for all mer innocents to be protected."

Now everyone around the table was interested in what Arianna had found in Whitney. Whitney knew it didn't come from her memories because she had no clue what was going on, but she was pretty sure it came from something deep inside of her. That was the only explanation she could come up with. Arianna was completely certain of what she was saying.

Arianna walked over to the door Whitney had entered and opened it. There, in the hallway, stood Trudy. She smiled and gave a small wave to Whitney. Whitney was beyond shocked and then a bit taken back by how much fear Trudy wasn't feeling. Did she not know where she was? Whitney would have been mad to see her friend in danger, but now the siren—and thus Trudy—were part of the night human world.

"I know I didn't ask you, but I had someone bring one of your siren here to show you the power you hold."

Trudy walked into the room at Turner's prompting as he got her a chair to sit in next to Whitney. Trudy sat down and gave Whitney her best brave smile even though her hands were clamped together to keep from shaking. Okay, she was terrified after all. That was a much more expected emotion. Whitney wasn't a fan of having people in her head and was more than thankful the king couldn't enter her mind, but for once she wished she could talk to her friend to reassure her it was safe and they would be fine. Well, at least she hoped they would be fine. She hadn't heard the beginning of what Arianna was telling everyone.

"So the Oceanids are a type of merperson. Why the siren didn't know that you are one is because no one has seen one for hundreds of years, and each Oceanid is different. It isn't like how the siren have green or blue tails. An Oceanid can be any color they want."

"Um." Trudy raised her hand. "I think I missed something. Are you saying Whitney isn't a siren?"

Smiling at Trudy, Arianna nodded. "I'm saying she's much more than a siren. Each of the merclans come from different Oceanids that once populated the Earth, but as they were not needed and had children to continue on taking care of their part of the water, they left. Loan is the one who's heard the most legends of them, but they supposedly come back in times of need, and that's why Whitney was able to turn into one. The siren blood used to save her turned her into what the mer world really needed."

Whitney nodded her head, but it still didn't make much sense. She was sitting before the night human council now because she needed help. She couldn't save anyone, let alone the island of siren that were going to be attacked any day. There was no way she could defeat all the enemies, and with Sam and his need to protect everyone, he would be in the front lines of the fight. She probably couldn't help him. Being a savior to the mer seemed like an unlikely reason she had a pink tail.

Arianna watched Whitney as she thought, and Whitney finally realized the blonde night human was listening into her thoughts again.

"I'd like to blame my train of thought going wild on my hair color," Whitney added, picking up a strand of her blond hair.

Arianna let out a small laugh. Then Whitney realized that insinuating her blonde hair made her lose track of things wasn't the best thing to do since she was talking to another blond. *Oops.*

"I can show you how you're going to save the mer," Arianna said. "All I need is for you to transform."

A fish out of water. That didn't seem like it was going to save anyone, but since Arianna seemed to have all the answers, Whitney wasn't about to doubt her. Taking only a second to straighten her legs, Whitney turned into her mer form and let her long pink tail drape in front of her.

"I need to borrow a scale," Arianna explained as she reached forward and plucked a scale from Whitney's tail.

The iridescent scale sparkled pink as Arianna held it carefully between her thumb and forefinger. It actually didn't hurt that bad to have one scale taken out of her skin, and where it had been was already covered as a new one grew in its place. At least that was good to know.

"And now I need to borrow your arm." Arianna moved over to Trudy, who held her right arm out for Arianna. Whitney wasn't sure if Trudy knew who Arianna was, but Trudy seemed to understand doing what she said was the only option. Then again, it might have been Andrew standing behind the table giving them a 'you have to behave' glare that did it.

Arianna pressed the scale to Trudy's arm and then waited. Whitney wasn't sure what they were waiting for, but all the people in the room watched expectantly. That was the great thing about night humans; they lived in such a weird world, no one questioned what she was doing.

"Try transforming," Arianna finally suggested.

Trudy turned into her green form, but this time something

unexpected happened. Instead of being the full fish monster she had been only the night before in the pool, she was half human just like Whitney and carried the same purple swirls across her upper body. Her tail was still green with flecks of pink every now and then, but she wasn't the same green siren she had been before she had come into the room.

"It worked," Arianna said. Of course, she realized it, too. She could see into Whitney's mind and see the difference. She must have shown the rest of the people in the room as they gasped in unison.

*'How is this possible?'* Trudy asked as she looked at her scale-free arms before feeling her own face. She was no longer a monster in her night human form.

Whitney was startled by the voice in her head. She just heard her friend. Whitney turned to Arianna for an explanation.

"She's part of your clan now, and just like the siren king, you'll be able to hear everyone in your clan," Arianna explained.

Whitney wanted to protest, but instead was caught by the wide grin of Loan as he looked at her from behind Trudy.

His dimples deepened in his brown skin, pulled so tight by his bright smile. "I knew my grandmother was right. I can't wait to have some good luck for a change."

## CHAPTER 5

**Sam was still** so disappointed Whitney hadn't met him the night before that he didn't sleep well. She was out there on land, running around trying to keep the siren safe. That was his job description, not hers. She should be safe on the island beside him, but instead, he sat up for hours worrying about her. As the sun hit the ocean and began its morning tune, Sam gave up sleeping completely and went to the pool to soak instead.

He couldn't help as his thoughts drifted to Whitney. He couldn't talk to her, but felt faint traces of emotion every now and then. She was scared, tired, and confused. That didn't seem like things were going very well. And siren, in general, did horrible the further inland they went. There wasn't a siren he knew that survived more than a few days inland. Whitney thought it was because they worried too much about water, but he had a feeling that it had more to do with their connection to the ocean. He trusted that she would stay safe, but he still worried that sometimes even the best fighter could lose.

Sinking down into the water, Sam felt for her. He had to know she was feeling safe at the moment and not scared as she had before. At least that much of the connection stayed alive. He wouldn't be able to bear it otherwise.

Day was coming, and soon the whole village would be up and training. They had preparations to do to keep the people unable to fight safe, and training to do with every able body who could. The king had finally told everyone on the island the truth that war was coming and Sam was happy he caved in and believed it himself. Now maybe they would stand a chance instead of being blind the moment it came. Sam just hoped that Whitney could figure things out before it did, and she would be beside him.

As he soaked in the lukewarm water, he finally realized Whitney was no longer scared. She was confused more than anything. What he would have given to be able to go into her mind and ask what was going on. Confused but not scared had to be a good sign. Confused meant she was safe enough to ponder something, whatever it was.

When the tingling started in his fin, Sam didn't look down. He had been going without a proper soak for too long, and his fin had to be rehydrating as he had been in the pool for over an hour already. He wasn't needed with the prepping that was happening now. Well, maybe he was needed, but he refused to help with anything until he heard from Whitney.

The tingling grew more intense, and he had to look and see what was going on. It didn't feel like when his father burned off his scales in punishment, but something was definitely happening. Sam opened his eyes and found his tail wasn't completely blue now. There were pink scales every now and then—pink scales that looked awfully similar to his mate's.

Hopping out of the pool suddenly and changing before he normally should have, he had to grab a towel to dry off since he was now soaking wet in his clothes. His new fin was too much of a surprise development. He wasn't going to meet with Whitney again until later, but he had to go try the ocean to see if he could talk to her. Something was going on, and he needed to know what it was.

Changing into dry shorts, Sam took off down the path to the ocean. Normally, he liked how secluded his house was and away from the ocean, but as he had to wind around the various houses and down the path to the sea, he was regretting not building closer like everyone else. He did his best to avoid anyone so he wouldn't have to stop, and that was a feat in itself. Sam reached the water's edge and was about to go in when he froze in place.

*'Hi, Sam,'* Whitney's voice rang in his head. *'I have something big I have to tell you.'*

**Whitney had been** assured that Cassie and Jared were keeping the siren safe in her absence, but she still wanted to be back with them. Instead, she had to stay around the night human council mansion, wherever it was, and get all the details of the pardon on the record. It was important but time-consuming. Actually, in reality, Whitney was using her time to enjoy the outdoor pool while the majority of the night humans slept and the council argued over every last dot in the pardon. It had given her some much needed time to talk to Sam. With their bond, he was now part of her new night human merfamily, and her connection was complete with him. She could speak to him at any time, which was a huge relief.

"So how'd he take it?" Trudy asked from the spot in the pool next to her. She was still admiring being a mer with a normal upper body. She hadn't gone under the water even once.

"About as well as I expected."

"Meaning Prince Sam ordered you to return back to the island. Otherwise he would come get you?" Trudy understood Sam quite well, but then again, he had been her prince all her life. Whitney had thought it was just a nickname, but it was really who he was.

"Wouldn't he be King Sam now that I get my own whole race of mer?" Whitney pondered, trying to make light of the situation. Having her own race meant nothing if the siren island was attacked.

"Oh, yeah, and I get to call you Your Royal Highness now, too," Trudy teased. Even her red curls remained in her mer form, and Whitney actually found it strange to see her friend as a normal mer. It was obvious that Trudy found it strange also, as she kept looking at her own skin when she talked instead of at Whitney.

"Do you think the other siren will be fine with this?" Whitney asked. She really hadn't taken that into consideration. The siren were pretty set in their ways and traditions, and she was basically breaking all of it. Making the greens into normal mer was bound to have consequences, but starting a whole new race was an even bigger change for all of them.

"I'll tell you the greens will be thrilled. Do you know how often we get called 'monster' and not just by the stray human that might see us in our mer form? The blues think it's funny to make fun of us, too. Like this, they can't make fun of me now. I am sure every green will be offering to join you as soon as they seen this. Yes, the greens will be happy."

"And the blues?"

Sam didn't seem happy or sad about what was going on. His main and only concern was that Whitney wasn't being treated badly or thrown in jail by the night human council. It took almost five minutes to get him to calm down enough after explaining that she had been to see the council and convince him that she really was safe. He was certain they were planning on killing her for the crimes of the mer in the past. He really couldn't believe the pardon. That was going to take time to get used to.

Trudy shrugged. "I can't imagine they'll be mad about joining the night human world legitimately. Every siren has to worry if they set foot on shore, and then you have to worry about how to get food without killing someone. Access to blood will be a plus none of the siren can complain about. And if they do have a problem, just don't let them join your new mer, and you don't have to worry about them." Trudy winked at Whitney.

It wasn't like Whitney completely got what her whole new mer clan was or how to make them. So excluding anyone at this point was a moot point. Arianna seemed to understand it way better than Whitney, and that was just by touching her. Whitney wondered if there was some sort of spell or hidden memories, or something like that she had accessed because it would be really great if Whitney could access them, too. It was just one more thing to ask about when she got the chance ... rather, if she got the chance. She had yet to see the council again.

As if she knew she was being thought of, Arianna appeared in the doorway into the mansion. Whitney hopped up on the side of the pool and transformed back into her human self.

"You know that's one trick I haven't found in any other night human," Arianna told her. Whitney scrunched her face as she was confused. "To be able to transform with your clothes on and then come back when you change back. When I transform, if my clothes are too tight, they rip to shreds. Then if I want to go back, I'll be stark naked."

"Oh that," Whitney replied. "I agree. Best trick ever. Skinwalkers shred their clothes, too. Now I never need to worry, unless I transform in water. Then I have wet clothes."

Arianna smiled and walked over to one of the lounge chairs on the deck of the pool. Ever the diligent friend, Trudy stayed in the water but moved to the far edge to give them privacy.

"We've wrapped up all the details. It looks like we have a complete pardon and we will immediately stock a blood bank for the siren that come to shore. We had to talk a bit with the night humans in Florida. It seems like there's very little land not claimed by at least one clan, and trust me, you don't want to get into land claimed by more than one. The town you showed me seems to be completely free for the siren to have. Are you sure that's enough?"

"Plenty. The siren prefer the island and the ocean anyway. We don't need a whole territory to claim for ourselves." That much was true. Beyond the students, none of the adults ever came back. Maybe they would now, but

Whitney doubted it. The island was their perfect home.

"We've claimed the land for the Oceanids clan. The one thing is the council wants to be able to tell good from bad mer. So they couldn't be swayed in this—all siren on land have to be part of your clan. If anyone refuses to join, they won't have the pardon. The pardon is only for the Oceanid clan, not the siren. Loan explained a bit more to us, and it was as I expected from your locked up memories. Oceanids are good. There's no evil in them, and anyone you claim as part of your clan will have to be good, too."

"As in, they don't kill humans?" Whitney clarified.

"For the most part that would disqualify someone, but there are other things that define evil. I have a feeling your scales will only stick to those that are good. The rest will still be hunted. So make sure to change everyone as soon as you can."

Whitney nodded. That made sense. And in reality, she didn't want an evil clan anyway. She could live with that ... especially since it wasn't really her choosing, her scales would choose. No one could call her unfair; it was beyond her control. Well, kind of.

"I didn't mean to peek, but I saw that the siren are in trouble. As a rule, night human clans don't interfere with other clans. I have no night humans who will step between a civil war. The council has offered to let you and any of your Oceanids stay here at the manor until it's done. You are one of a kind, and if you go back and get killed, then the siren will have no chance at life on land." Arianna watched her like she was waiting for some sort of retort.

Instead, all Whitney felt was shock. Never once did she think she would stay out of the battle. There were too many people on the island that she wanted to protect. And there was Sam. She couldn't just leave him. He was her mate. That alone bound her to the island. Her life was already his.

"Your friend Cassie knows how to transfer mate bonds in case someone dies. If your mate were to die, there's one council member I'm more than certain would volunteer to keep you alive," Arianna added quietly, knowing or maybe listening into what Whitney was feeling.

Was she serious? Did Arianna just expect she would leave Sam behind?

"Would you take a new mate?"

Whitney glanced over Arianna's shoulder to her dark-haired mate who stood leaning against the building. It seemed like he didn't let her out of his sight, ever.

Arianna glanced back, and her face spread into the biggest smile Whitney had ever seen on someone. When she turned back, she tried to keep her face neutral but failed. Whitney didn't need an answer. A girl didn't look that way at a guy without loving them with their whole heart. And though Sam was thousands of miles away, he made Whitney feel the exact same happiness.

"And would you let your mate run off to battle without you?" Whitney added.

This time Arianna didn't turn around. "I could never leave him even if I wanted to, and there's no way I'd let him fight without me."

"Exactly. I need to get back to my siren and get them home. War is coming, and hopefully, my status as an Oceanid will bring luck like Loan seems to think."

Arianna nodded. "I figured you would say as much, but I had to try. You don't realize how special you really are. Night humans don't just appear out of nowhere, but that's exactly how you came to be. You might have just been a girl before all of this, but your mate gave you a gift beyond just coming back to the home you were meant to be in. You are something no one has ever been, or probably will be again. You are a legend coming to life."

Whitney felt the gravity in her words. She really couldn't explain why she was different than the rest of the siren, but now she knew. It made everything fall into place, and even the weird feelings of dread were now explained. Her life had changed when Sam turned her, but she never could have guessed he was turning her into something no one had seen in hundreds of years. Whitney wasn't sure it was ever going to feel real, but that wasn't going to stop her. She needed to get home and help any way she could.

"Good luck in protecting your siren. I've contacted the hunters, and they are willing to send some hunters with you to help out, but that's all I can do. Make sure you change all your siren before you meet them, though, because they have been told any mer without a pink scale on their arm is fair game to kill."

Whitney nodded as Arianna stood back up with a grace that made her seem like she was dancing. Arianna began to walk toward her waiting mate, and his eyes never left her.

"I really wish you good luck, and I hope to see you again one day. I hope Loan's stories are as true as you hope and you can bring the siren the luck they need." And with a curt nod from Arianna, she left Whitney and Trudy at the pool.

"Time to head back?" Trudy asked as she swam over and hopped out of the pool. Obviously, she was listening into the conversation and ready to get back to the real world.

"Time to plan our way to help the siren, starting by changing everyone into an Oceanid that we can find."

Trudy held up her hand to give her a high five on that one. All the siren waiting with Cassie were greens, and Whitney agreed they would all be thrilled to be changed. But Whitney didn't give her the high five she was waiting for.

"But how again do we get back?" Whitney wasn't even sure how Trudy came to the manor, let alone where they even were.

Trudy started laughing and pointed to her purse sitting on a table.

"We call Cassie to pick us up. Glad she told at least one of us. I'm not sure what state we are even in, let alone city."

And with that Whitney laughed along with her friend. Here she was this all-powerful mer, and she had to agree.

She had no clue where she was, where her siren were, or how to get back to anyone. It was a good thing Trudy had come to the council, too. Whitney needed that laugh and smile. And what better person to laugh with, but a friend?

**Whitney looked around** the bare hotel room. It was a much better place than the dive they first were in. The paint wasn't peeling, and the bed quilts didn't smell funky, but it was still not the five-star resorts Whitney preferred. Not that it mattered. She was back with her siren and had explained what had happened. All six of the waiting siren were happy to hear the news and immediately wanted to join her. Thankfully, as she had expected, they were all deemed good enough and the scale stuck to them. They didn't have time to try out their new siren forms, but they were all excited to see how true Trudy had been when describing it.

It was time for Cassie to go home and for the sirens to find out who was sent for help. With hundreds if not thousands of mer getting ready to attack the island, Whitney hoped it was an army. One hunter was worth at least ten or more night humans because they had advanced strength and endurance, but she needed a bunch if they were going to win the war.

Cassie waited by a tree that was just outside the hotel.

"I hate to leave you now. It's like they just gave us permission to be friends, but I have to go. Not fair," Cassie complained, her dark hair pulled back into a ponytail. She shook her tail as she pouted.

"And when we get done with all of this we can still be friends. War doesn't change our friendship. Heck, I don't know anything that could really stop us from being friends. When it is all done, we will catch up on everything. I can't wait for you to meet Sam," Whitney added.

"So mystery guy does have a name." Cassie nudged Whitney's shoulder. Now that Sam was safe in the night human world, Whitney was absolutely going to show him around and introduce him to everyone.

"And you can't deny going back. I'm sure Nate is going crazy without you, and since your uncle ordered it, you have to go." Whitney hugged her friend. She really didn't want her to leave. Everything always felt like it fit into place with Cassie around. Now she was going to have to force everything into place.

"I know, but I still wish you were there like old times," Cassie replied.

"I don't miss being able to hear the whole skinwalker clan in my head. Do you know that it is like to have someone able to tell you what to do all the time? It was a pain, and to hear only voices of guys ... That was torture also. Now I have my own clan, and I plan to stay out of everyone's head."

"Except Sam's," Cassie added in a sing-song voice.

Whitney smacked her best friend in the arm. "You can't say his name like that. He's the lead singer in a rock band."

Cassie covered her mouth when she began to giggle.

"I'm serious," Whitney added, and her friend's hand dropped from her mouth to show she was shocked.

"Like as in a real rock band?"

"Yes. That's how the siren got money on land. Sam's band is doing pretty good. I promise when this is all done I'll even take you to one of his concerts."

Cassie reached forward and hugged Whitney. "I'm going to miss you. We have to get back together and get all caught up. I've missed so much in your life over the past few months. I wish you would have come to me sooner."

That was the one regret for Whitney. She should have gone to Cassie sooner, but she didn't want to get her in trouble. She could see now that their friendship was stronger than ever, and she wouldn't have been in trouble. Cassie would have kept her secret, and Whitney was ashamed she doubted that for a minute. Now she didn't need to worry. Nothing was going to keep them apart again, as long as the whole war thing ended up in her favor. There was only that little detail.

Cassie put her hand on the tree, and the large cat Jared walked up and wrapped his body against her side. Without another word, Cassie melted away with her cat, and Whitney was left to play her new role of leader. Somehow she was supposed to know what to do next. And she needed to figure things out fast. Sam wasn't sure how much longer the mer barricading the island would be happy to sit and wait. And he didn't know why Tim hadn't shown them the way in yet.

As Cassie left, a car pulled into the parking lot. Whitney waited tensely while the car door opened and a middle-aged woman stepped out. From the driver's seat, a teen boy emerged. They both looked straight at Whitney and nodded. With impeccable timing, the hunters were starting to arrive.

"Hi. The council told us that we should meet a night human here with a pink mark on her arm. Since you have that mark, I'm assuming you are the one we need to talk to about our new assignment?" the lady said as she moved closer. How she saw the pink mark over twenty feet away was beyond Whitney.

"Yeah. Hi. I'm Whitney. I'm the leader of a new clan of night humans called the Oceanids." She held out her hand, but the lady made no move to shake it. Pulling her hand back, she continued. "I've been given the right to pardon any good siren, but the problem is I can't get to them. Their island is surrounded by a ton of mer clans."

"So we're off to kill fish?" the lady asked, like the whole pardon part didn't interest her at all.

"Yes, we're going to fight with mer," Whitney replied, unsure what to make of her. She was petite, maybe five-foot-three and old enough to sport wrinkles at the corner of her eyes. She obviously didn't have wrinkles from smiling—more likely from the permanent scowl across her face. She nodded to Whitney.

"I'll go make my plans on which weapons to pick up on

the way," she replied and went back to the car. The teenage boy was left behind, staring at the ground.

"Um, hi. I'm Whitney," she tried again, offering her hand to the teen. It took him a moment to realize she was talking to him.

"Oh, hi. I'm Kevin, and my mother is Claudia. I know she's a bit intense, but you'll find she's good at being a hunter. She'll be a great asset to your hunting expedition." The crew-cut kid gave her a big smile.

"Hunting expedition?"

"Yes, the hunter's council got a call from the night human council that there was a congregation of illegal mer that needed to be killed. We were sent to help." Now the boy seemed as confused as Whitney.

Suddenly it made more sense. As she was waiting for more to show up, more weren't coming. This wasn't going to work. They had sent a hunter and her teen. There was no way just these two were going to be any help.

"There's no more coming, are there?" Whitney had to confirm her suspicion.

"More? Hunters are all trained to handle at least a dozen night humans at a time. Why would you need more hunters?"

Whitney rubbed her forehead. This wasn't going to help at all. How in the world was she going to help or make it back home unless there were more hunters? Two hunters was a great start, but that was all it was, just a start. They needed more help.

"There are thousands of mer in the waters around the siren island. Thousands. And I have seven untrained siren teens with me. One hunter isn't going to help much with that, and basically, you would be going on a suicide mission." Whitney shook her head. She thought being an Oceanid meant having luck, but maybe that luck was only for someone who touched her mer lines and not for her. Well, that stunk. What was the purpose of being special if it made no difference?

"That's impossible. Our records have the mer population of being up to maybe a hundred at the most. If my mother takes on a group at a time, she will do fine with a hundred."

Whitney's eyes bugged. *Their information?* What the heck. They didn't know anything. Each race had more than a thousand mer each, and there were more than a dozen races. *Maybe a hundred?* This wasn't going to work.

"There are currently 1,374 siren residing on the island. While that might seem like a lot, it's actually smaller than most of the mer clans. Not all of the people in a clan will be fighting, just the men and some women in their prime, but there will be hundreds if not thousands in the battle. I'm not lying to you. That's the truth, and one hunter may help, but like I said, it would be a suicide mission for them."

Claudia returned, and she was staring at Whitney like she was trying to decide whether to believe her or not. The hunters didn't seem like the type to admit they were wrong and their information on mer, in general, was not very accurate.

"My night human family is on that island. I've lived on the island and have seen it with my own eyes. There were way more mer than you could have ever imagined." Whitney tried her best to stress to the hunter and her son that she was telling the truth. She needed them to believe her.

That news didn't seem to sit well with Claudia. Her frown returned, and she marched back to her car, opened the trunk, and began removing more weapons that she piled on the ground.

"What is she doing?" Whitney whispered to her son Kevin.

"Probably cataloging everything we have with us, and counting how many more weapons we need to go pick up." He shrugged like he wasn't completely sure either.

"So there really is no one else coming?" Whitney had to start making her own plans. The hunters weren't being very helpful.

"No one else. We really believed there were only a hundred at most left. My mom was the only one dispatched for this mission."

Whitney nodded and began to pace in the parking lot. There had to be someone to call that would be willing to help and turn the tide of the coming war to her side. She wanted the chance for the siren to be free. She considered the skinwalkers, but it wasn't their fight. As Arianna had explained, and Whitney knew too well, night humans stayed out of each other's politics. It had to be that way, or there would be another night human war. What Whitney needed was day humans strong enough to fight, but it didn't help when she only had two. That just wasn't enough. And she didn't exactly want to lead two complete strangers off to their deaths, either. The teen had to be younger than her. He deserved to at least have a few more decades to his life instead of dying in a feud of night humans.

"And if we call for more?" Whitney asked as she came in front of the teen again.

"They won't send help. They won't believe additional hunters are needed no matter what you tell them. They truly believe there are only a hundred left. Sending more would be unnecessary. The only way backup hunters would come was if you were a hunter and could tell them that. They only trust each other, and sorry, but you're a night human. One with an interest in saving the island of mer on top of things. You wouldn't be trustworthy to a hunter."

Whitney stared at Kevin. That was it. She might not be trustworthy to the hunter's council, but she was trustworthy to one hunter and her brother in particular.

"Tell your mom to pack everything away. I need to make a phone call, and then go find myself a few more hunters to bring to the party."

Whitney walked away, leaving the teen boy with his mother. She knew who she needed to call, and she knew

Jade would believe her. Now she just had to break the news that she was a night human and hopefully be forgiven by her friends. Better yet, she would call Jax. He already knew, and he also knew that they'd messed with Jade and Rommy's minds before the hunters left. She'd leave it up to him to explain it all and take their anger, because she knew they were both going to be upset. Hopefully, they had enough connections to bring more people with, and at least Jax's mother's eternal hate of the mer would more than likely drive her to not want to miss the fight.

Maybe, just maybe, Whitney did have a bit of luck. The hunters moving to town and befriending her was more than coincidence. There might have just been some good fortune in her meeting the exact people she would need to help her.

# CHAPTER 6

**Sam stood on** the shore, watching for any non-siren getting past the barrier. Nothing was happening. It was all intact. He could see the shimmer of the magical barrier, but it wasn't going to hold. They were up to something, and he wanted more than anything to go find out what. But he had promised Whitney he'd stay back from the fighting for now. If he got killed, it would kill her, too, and all chance of asylum for the siren would be gone. He wanted to protect and save everyone, and right now the best way to do that was to stay back and let someone else investigate.

Nic dove into the water near him and gave him a wave as he took off to see what was going on. Sam wanted to be there beside his brother, but a promise was a promise.

Whitney had now been checking in with him almost every hour. He was delighted to find that the bond went two ways and he could talk to her when he needed to also. It was hard to hold back, though. He knew she was busy gathering hunters and making plans. Otherwise, he would be talking to her as he waited.

Sam was excited to begin a new life where they weren't hunted. It actually seemed too good to be true, and he hadn't yet told his father about it. What difference would it make if they died before it came to pass? For now, he wanted everyone to focus on their jobs. Everyone between the ages of sixteen and fifty were training to fight. The mothers and the children were busy fortifying the safe points in town and prepping everything for evacuation if it became an option. They were going to be ready.

Something was happening in the water. Sam wasn't close enough to see, but something was going on. He waited on the pier and was going to decide what to do when his brother, Ken, came barreling down and jumped in before Sam could ask. That wasn't a good sign. Ken was good with thinking and problem solving, not fighting. If he was going in the water, then something was really wrong. Without hesitating, Sam jumped in after Ken. He wasn't going to let his one logical brother get hurt before the war even started. They needed his smarts if they were going to stand any chance.

Underwater, Sam easily caught up to his brother. Ken didn't look back at him as he raced off to a specific spot. Ken suddenly came to a halt. Sam stopped beside his brother and glanced around. There had to be a reason why he stopped. Ken didn't do anything without a reason. What was his brother up to?

Nic hadn't been the nicest brother to Sam, but none of them had. Sam was the youngest, and while he didn't notice, his father favored him. Sam believed that being sent to another ocean for his coming of age journey was because his father didn't want him, but it turned out to be the opposite. His father had enough faith in him getting home on his own. His father was proud of him, and to be able to have a son who had accomplished that made him prouder, even if he never showed that to Sam. Sam understood why his brothers, including Nic, had treated him badly for most of his life, but that didn't mean they weren't his brothers. And now even more so, he trusted them, especially Nic, who had trained Whitney to fight and take care of herself to the point that Sam didn't really need to worry about her on land.

As Sam saw what they stopped for, his heart sank. At the bottom of the ocean, Nic was clamped in a mer trap that was similar to what people used to hunt animals on land. His whole lower half was chomped through with the large metal teeth. The outside mer couldn't physically pass the border, but they found a way to start the fight without doing that. Sam moved to swim down and try to help Nic, but Nic shook his head. Reaching out, Ken grabbed Sam before he could move forward.

Ken seemed to have a silent conversation with Nic before nodding and pulling Sam back to the pier. Sam could have fought Ken, but it seemed that Ken knew more about what was going on. Once he had the details, he'd be back. He gave one last look at Nic and Nic gave him a salute. Sam had to hope that wouldn't be the last time he saw his brother alive. Siren could live indefinitely underwater, but he wasn't sure Nic would live without the blood that was slowly leaking from him.

Even if they weren't ready, the war was starting. Sam needed to be prepared to lose more people, but losing Nic would be hard. He'd discovered he liked his brothers after all.

**Whitney felt Sam's** pain across the bond and wanted to ask what was going on, but she couldn't. She was busy with her own problems. When Sam had taken her to the island near the mer, he had used a specific boat company. Now that company was nowhere to be found. Even after searching the Internet she still didn't have any clues. And since she had been asleep when Sam moved her onto the boat, she wasn't sure what city the port they came out of was even in.

Currently, Whitney was on her third city, and they were driving through searching for the boat company. She had been a little too focused on Sam the only time she rode on the boat to completely recall the name of the company, which probably would have made things easier. At least she could remember the logo, even if she forgot the writing on it. Now she just needed to find that logo.

"So you're really not mad at me for everything?" Whitney asked for the tenth time. When Jade had left town, Sam had wiped her memories from being kidnapped and then the fight between the mer clans.

"I don't remember being kidnapped by a mermaid, so I don't hold a grudge against them. Nope, not mad at all. It seemed like something I don't need to remember, or it wasn't that fun anyway. Now if you took away going to Sam's concert, that I would have been mad about." Jade winked at Whitney. Her hair was currently a deep blue-green color that almost matched her name. "Do you remember that cute bouncer?" Yes, he was hard to forget, particularly since he'd had arms the size of Whitney's thighs and scared the crap out of her when he scowled at someone. He wasn't Whitney's type, but he seemed to be Jade's. "I got his number, and he told me to call anytime I was back in the area." Jade winked at Whitney, who just shook her head. Jade's concern about dating a guy was strange considering they were looking to go into a life-threatening fight soon enough.

"I'm still sorry about the whole wiping your memories thing. I didn't want to take away any memories from you, but Sam said your mother wouldn't have given up since she saw his father."

"Yeah, they have some feud going back a couple decades. I never knew it was Sam's dad she was mad at. We knew there was this guy she was set on killing, and that's why she volunteered for every case with a possible mermaid, but I have no idea what it's about. She never told us why she hates the mer in particular, but then again she doesn't tell us much anyways." Jade brushed her short hair with her fingers.

"I asked Sam, and he has no clue beyond your mother taking a child from his father's best friend, causing his friend to disappear from grief. Nothing more than that, and I've never seen his father ever once mention your mother in the past months I've been on the island. It's like they have their own little world where they hate each other, but when they aren't there, it doesn't exist." Whitney pulled into yet another marina.

"Man, you have to tell me all about facing the night

human council. That's some serious business. Did you know they deal out punishment instantly? Like no last call to tell your loved ones good-bye? And they think hunters have no soul. At least we understand being human and saying goodbye."

Whitney didn't know that and was thankful she didn't. While she didn't expect they would keep her alive for being an outlawed night human, she did think it was going to include some sort of prison sentence and a farewell phone call at least.

"What if they change their minds? What can you do if you've already killed someone?"

At this Jade laughed. "A night human changing its mind? Impossible! If you ask any night human out there, they will explain to you they are perfect and don't make any mistakes." Jade stepped out of the car with Whitney and finally noticed her friend had not replied. "Shoot. I'm sorry about that. It's going to take a long time to get used to you being a night human. You just seem no different than before."

Whitney shrugged. "I'm not different because the whole time you knew me I was a night human. Sam had changed me before you moved to town. But the thing is, if you asked my friend Cassie, I've never changed even from skinwalker to human to mer. I'm still me."

"Which is a testament to how strong of a person you are," Jade added with a meek smile. "Not everyone can become hungry for blood, and remain so innocent and nice."

Whitney smiled before realizing she hadn't fed in a long time, and yet she still wasn't hungry. Maybe this was something new with being an Oceanid, whatever that was. She had to hope that was the case and it would stay that way because she didn't have time to get hungry. She still didn't have any more details, but she was anxious to get back and ask Ken all he knew on the subject of Oceanids. Of everyone, she knew he would be the most interested from all his book reading.

"You've never met the skinwalkers I'm guessing. There isn't blood hunger, and they're all normal people. I think because you were raised as a hunter, all the night humans you ever met are the bad ones. There are actually a lot of good ones, and my mer clan is going to be all good. I promise you that. The only time you'll be coming to see me is to take a vacation on my awesome tropical mer island."

Jade held up her hand to give her a high five.

"And I can't wait. My mother is pushing me to do the final tests to be a full-fledged hunter, but it's stressful. Once I am, though, Jax can be my apprentice instead of Mom's, and we can leave on our own."

Whitney's eyes went big. Her friend was just graduating from high school, and here she was talking about going off on her own. That sounded scary. Whitney was on her own, but not really. She had Sam, and even now wanted to check in on him. Something was going on at the island, but there was nothing she could do to help until she could get closer.

"And your mom's good with that?"

Rommy seemed to have control issues, and Whitney was happy to be off searching marinas with just Jade. She wasn't sure she could survive another car ride with the lady. Heck, on their way back to the coast, she had driven the van to follow the hunter group and lost her on more than one occasion because of Rommy's fast driving. It was a good thing they had gotten directions before leaving.

Whitney and Jade walked down the wooden walkway to the pier. It was yet another stop, and she was hopeful they would find what they were looking for.

"I think she's excited. She spent most of my childhood complaining that we weighed her down and she was missing her prime hunting time." Whitney's face dropped. "But it's okay. Really," Jade tried to reassure her. "All the hunters are like that. They complain about their kids to their kids, but they do love us. But they love the hunt just as much. I really don't get it yet, but my mom keeps telling me I will." Jade shrugged. "Yes, hunting is exciting. I mean, it is life and death after all. But it isn't better than life. I like going to school and hanging out with Jax. I wish I could go to college, but it isn't in the cards for me."

Whitney paused as Jade stopped to stare at the sign. This was it. She remembered it perfectly, the round logo with a V right in the middle of it. Whitney had found their boat. Now she needed to find someone on it.

"This is it," Whitney said as Jade stopped beside her and looked at the sign. "I'm going to go onboard and see if anyone is around."

Jade nodded. "I'll call my mother and get the crew ready."

Whitney nodded back to her. Jade stepped a few feet away to make the call and Whitney walked over to the boat. There was a small shack next to the boat that listed the trips it went on. She wasn't sure which destination they needed and each day of the week went to different places. As she stared at the sign, someone came up and stood beside her. Turning and expecting to find Jade, she was surprised at the young man beside her.

"Looking for a trip?" he asked, eyeing her over like he knew her secret.

"Yes. I've been on this boat once before, though I'm just not completely sure where I want to go," Whitney replied, thinking she should contact Sam as that would be the easiest.

Jade walked up to them and pulled back her sleeve. The large tattoo on her forearm was completely visible.

"We're looking to go to the island you drop off night humans on," Jade told the man boldly. Whitney's eyes shot open. Night humans were supposed to stay secret to the general public, and Jade was being more than forward.

The guy didn't flinch and just nodded.

"How many will I be transporting, hunter?" he asked. Okay, obviously the guy was in the loop, but how Jade knew was beyond Whitney. Now she just had more questions for her friend.

"We have eight night humans and eight hunters, and we would like to leave as soon as we can," Jade replied, not even blinking while looking at the man. Her tone was more serious than it had been all afternoon.

He nodded to her and then walked back to the shack, pulling the door shut before going down the walkway to the waiting boat. "I should be able to get my crew here within the hour," he called over his shoulder, not turning around.

Jade nodded to the man's back.

"Let's go back to the car to get my stuff and wait for everyone. They should be here as soon as my mom stops to get more weapons. To say she's excited is an understatement, I hope you know." Only a hunter would be happy to go off to the middle of a night human war excited. Six more hunters wasn't exactly the backup army Whitney thought would help, but by having Rommy there counted as having a dozen hunters. Whitney was ready to take her chances with those numbers.

Eight hunters and eight untrained teenage siren. It wasn't the best plan, but it was better than what she had started with. She was going to get back to the island to wait now, and she was excited to be close to Sam. Things on the island were getting worse, and something more had happened. She didn't need to be able to see things with her own eyes to know that it was bad and they needed to start working on their latest plan. As much as the siren had feared the hunters for decades, Whitney was glad to have them beside her. Rommy had a plan to start trimming the mer down before the real war began, and it actually sounded like something they could do as they waited.

Smiling, Whitney watched her friend pull out bags of weapons. Weeks ago she was happy to have visited Jade's house and come out alive because she feared the hunters, and now she was standing beside them getting ready to go into battle. Her decision to face the night human council had changed everything. Whitney hoped she could keep making the right choices like that, and was beginning to think maybe her Oceanid blood was lucky after all. It would be perfect if her luck continued until after the battle, and she was able to give the siren a new life in the night human world instead of outside it.

**The boat ride** was much longer than Whitney remembered, but then again, she had been asleep for part of it the first time. Actually, she didn't know how long she had been asleep. There was the small detail of how spending time with Sam made time fly by. Example being that the past couple months were really nothing more than a blur now. She wanted to remember every moment, but time went so fast.

Jade had explained that the captain of the boat was what they called a nur, or a night human sympathizer. There was a whole group of day humans that were into helping out night humans for their blood. The way Jade explained it, they were mostly junkies for the fix of the power night human blood gave them, but some, like the captain, found night humans to be the best allies—which explained her initial hostile behavior toward him. Either way, the tattoo on his neck told Jade who he was and that she could be direct with him. One more thing Whitney needed to learn about.

As the large sightseeing boat anchored at the island, Whitney and the other mer had to hide in the hulls of the rowboats as the hunters made their way to the shore. They weren't sure if the mer were watching the island or not, but it was best to keep the siren hidden.

Whitney lay on a tarp while Jax was rowing the first boat to shore.

"So were they mad when you told them?" Whitney asked. It was the first time she'd been alone with him since they met up the day before.

Jax laughed. "Mad? My sister and mother getting mad? No, never. They don't ever get mad." He laughed again, but Whitney didn't. She was worried that they would take out their anger on him since he seemed to be immune to the siren. He grinned down at her. "Okay, fine. Yes, they were mad, but nothing more than normal. They walk around mad. Yesterday, before you called, Jade was mad that the mac and cheese in the house wasn't the white kind, and she was going to have to eat yellow fake cheese. Come on. What *don't* they get mad about?"

"I mean more than normal," Whitney clarified.

"No. They both figured something happened when we met up with the mer, and their minds had been messed with, but I was right that once they had a body, they'd ease up a bit. It's all about the kill with them. Oh well. I would have been mad if I were them, but what can you do?"

Jax kept rowing. It wasn't far from the anchored boat to the shore, but Jax was taking his time to see the scenery. He was taking Whitney to the island first so that they could scope out the place before anyone else came ashore.

"Jade said you're going to be her apprentice now," Whitney continued, trying to keep the conversation going. What she really wanted was to be was sitting up with Jax and keeping a lookout for mer, but that wasn't an option with her hair back to being blond. They easily could be looking for her, too.

Jax shrugged. "I guess."

"Still not fair that you can't be a hunter also," Whitney added. Full hunter status was only given to females. Jax was only allowed to apprentice, which did stink. He was a really good shot, and from the stories Jade told, he was as good as she was at hand-to-hand combat. But he didn't have the extra hunter skills and strength to make it easier.

"My mother would tell you life isn't fair, but I get the feeling you already know that."

Whitney smiled at that. She had complained to Jax a lot

in the short time he had lived in her town. Something about him just made her trust him, and she got the feeling that because he reminded her of home with Cassie and their best friend Owen, she might have been more talkative than normal with him being new. Somehow he knew all long she wasn't completely human, but he never told his mother or sister. That alone made her trust him completely.

"Why didn't you tell them about us?" Whitney finally asked. She really wanted to know.

Jax shrugged as he continued to row. "What was I going to tell them? There are more mer in this town than anyone thought? Or that most of those kids in school are mer? Oh, and by the way, Jade, you know that one girl you like at school? She's a mer, too, and you need to kill her. That would have crushed Jade. And I knew you weren't who we were looking for. You were too good to be the one killing off humans."

How the heck did he know her that well? They were friends and all, but he saved her life. After all, she was an outlawed night human. If he had told the hunters, there would have been nothing she could do, and with Sam stuck on the island, he wouldn't have been able to save her.

"Whit, don't believe everything my sister says about night humans. It isn't as cut and dry as she tries to make it out to be. All the hunters do that to make themselves feel better about killing people. They have to. Otherwise, they will question every life they take. The fact of the matter is, every night human they kill is a person. Just because you drink blood doesn't make you evil."

Whitney smiled. She was glad she got to know Jax, and even happier he wasn't what she thought hunters were like.

The boat hit the sand, and Jax smiled as Whitney was jostled beneath him.

"Now the fun part," he told her, reaching down to wrap her in the tarp. It was not the fun part for her. She wasn't fond of being carried around, but being carried around like a wrapped up hotdog was even worse. She wouldn't even be able to see where he was walking.

"If you drop me ..." she threatened him as he placed a piece over her face.

Jax simply laughed as he stood up and hauled her over his shoulder like she weighed nothing. Making his way across the sand, Whitney had nothing to look at but the bright yellow grains as that was all she could see. After what seemed like at least twenty minutes of being wrapped in the hot, unbreathable tarp, Jax set her down on the ground. They were within the tree line and hidden from any eyes that might still be in the water watching them. Whitney jumped up as Jax took the tarp and hung it at the edge of the tree line like a curtain to indicate where they were.

Contrary to all his joking, Jax was actually a complete gentleman. She knew she didn't need to worry about him, but she couldn't help but threaten him. He was too good at playing the brother part that he even felt a bit like a brother to her.

Whitney closed her eyes to do her job. With her enhanced new Oceanid senses, she could feel every kind of mer perfectly. There were dots along the water surrounding the island, but they kept moving as if the island meant nothing to them. And the best part was the island was completely mer free. Not a single mer was on the island anywhere. They would be safe for now to make camp.

Whitney opened her eyes and looked at Jax. "None on the island, and no one in the waters tracking us. It's safe to bring everyone ashore, but I'd still keep the greens hidden just in case they catch anyone's attention."

Jax nodded and walked back to his waiting rowboat. He was on a mission now, and much more serious than he was just moments before in the boat.

Whitney stayed in the trees, which were out of the line of sight from the shore, and waited. It wouldn't take long to get everyone to their new home for the next few days, but beyond that, she wasn't sure what else they could do. Rommy had a plan to sit and lure the mer to the island in small groups and take care of them. That was one way to spend their time, and would be pretty useful, but Whitney felt like she needed to do more.

*'Sam?'* she finally called out to him. *'We made it to the island.'*

There was silence back, so she waited. She knew he was fine physically, but in the middle of an argument or something with his father. When his anger finally shut off, she tried again.

*'Sam, what's going on?'*

*'Sorry I didn't answer right away,'* he apologized.

*'Sam?'* Whitney knew he was avoiding the conversation. She didn't want to pry into his mind to find out the truth, but if she needed to, she would.

*'Nic went to check the barrier and got caught in a trap,'* Sam finally replied.

*'Trap? As in they took him?'* Whitney had no clue what he meant. He sent her a mental picture of his brother. It wasn't what she expected. *'Oh, no.'*

*'I want to go get him out of there and get him help, but my father refuses. He said I might get caught, so he can't risk letting me. He isn't concerned about my brother. He expects me to just sit and let Nic bleed out in the bottom of the ocean.'*

Whitney could feel Sam's pain. It wasn't fair, but the king was right. There was no indication that there were any more traps, but she had a very good feeling that Nic wasn't accidentally caught in one. He'd been the one training her. He was good, very good, in the water. He wouldn't have walked into one unless it was hidden well, and who was to say there weren't more of them, also hidden? It wasn't safe for Sam to attempt to rescue him.

*'So they can't cross the barrier, but they can send traps across?'* Whitney finally understood what was going on.

*'Seems so,'* Sam answered.

Sam sounded so defeated. It was time to change the subject. Whitney didn't want to keep him focused on the one thing he couldn't do anything about, and she needed his help elsewhere, anyway.

*'We are at the island, and the hunters are coming ashore as we talk. Rommy thinks they can take out up to fifteen mer at a time each. While that helps, it won't win the war. I feel like I have to do more, and I'm missing something. Like somehow there's a way that I can get us more allies in this fight. We need more bodies on our side.'*

Sam seemed to be on the same page. He agreed that what the hunters were planning would help, but it wasn't going to stop what was coming to the island. They needed to be able to reduce the direct hit once it came, but taking out fifteen mer every few hours wasn't going to dent their ranks enough to make them rethink attacking the island. Whitney followed his train of thought.

*'But what about if they were attacked by another clan? If we split their forces, then would the siren stand a chance of defending the island?'*

It was the question Whitney had been pondering all day.

Sam's anger over his brother was gone, and he was getting where Whitney was going with everything. They didn't need to share any images; they were on the same page in their thoughts.

*'There's one clan that hasn't joined either side, right?'* Whitney needed confirmation that it was still so.

*'The Selkie,'* Sam answered. *'If you can get the Selkie to join us, then we might have enough of a diversion to do this.'*

That's exactly what Whitney was hoping he would say. Now the question was, could she offer them a great enough incentive to join? Something was keeping them out so far, and she had to guess they didn't have a reason to help either side.

*'You don't have anything to barter with,'* Sam replied to

her thoughts.

*'Oh, but I do,'* she answered. She had something to barter with the whole mer world. *'I can give them freedom from being hunted. I can give them freedom in the night human world.'*

And for once in many days she felt optimism from Sam. Her plan was a good one, and she was happy to see he could agree. She was worried he would tell her it wouldn't work or it was too dangerous, but there was hope now. He was actually liking her plan. He was optimistic, and so was she.

*'I'll show you where they live, and you'll have to get to them as soon as you can. I don't know how long the barrier is going to hold since they now can get things across it.'*

Whitney nodded as she watched two hunters carry her green siren into the dense forest where she was waiting. They would get the war started without the mer world knowing. She had to assume she was doing enough and not missing something that could help. She was going to do everything she could to make her ideas work. She had to, and she had to hope her new Oceanid status would bring them the luck they needed.

## CHAPTER 7

**The hunters and** siren had their plan ready, and Whitney stood just beyond the tree line, hidden in the foliage to be sure it would work. Trevor was the youngest siren with them, but according to all of them, he was also the fastest one. He was being sent out to lure a mer onto land. They had found the perfect spot that had a river going inland, and right there they set up a camp full of hunters. They kept their hunter marks covered and got a bonfire going. Pretending to have a party in full motion was going to be the distraction to get the unsuspecting mer on land.

Trevor dove into the stream and headed out to sea. It wasn't going to take him long to find someone, and Whitney waited anxiously. She hated to see a kid who was barely fourteen being used as bait, but if everyone was correct, he would have the best chances of surviving. Whitney used her new senses as leader of the Oceanids to watch him as he made his way farther away from the island shores. It wouldn't take long before one of the passing mer saw him, and she was correct, as he soon hurried back the way he came. He would be quick enough to make it back without any trouble. She trusted him to stay safe.

As the unsuspecting mer passed the group of hunters, he stealthily climbed out of the river. Pursuing the lonely siren was going to take second place to grabbing an easy snack, just as they had predicted. The mer came closer to the group where they sat around the fire, drinking what appeared to be beer, but was just water.

"You will leave here and return with ten friends to feast on these humans without telling anyone where you are going. Make sure to not be followed," Trudy commanded the clueless mer. Her voice was not as strong as a blue, but it was strong enough to make any other mer do as she told.

His eyes glazed over and he, rather noisily, hopped into the river and back out to sea. It didn't take him long to find other mer, and soon enough they were all stealthily coming out of the water. Whitney kept her distance as she watched. She wanted to protect the new family she had just made, but she had to be sure they would be fine on their own for her to be able to leave them. Only if they got in trouble, would she step in.

And it seemed she wasn't needed. In fact, beyond luring the mer to land and making them get more mer to come back, it seemed like the young siren, now Oceanids, were not needed either. They stood back and watched also as the hunters handled the mer they had lured to the island. Whitney was happy to see that her charges wouldn't be doing any of the fighting, and possibly getting hurt or killed.

"See, what did I tell you?" Jax said as he stood beside Whitney. His job was to pick off any mer trying to make a run for it with his rifle. As everyone suspected, the mer thought the humans would be an easy treat, and not a single one ran for it. It seemed like Jax wasn't going to have much to do.

"Jax," Rommy called to him before they could talk more. Jax jogged down to his mother and started to help throw the mer bodies into the already roaring fire. Once the evidence was hidden enough, they would try to lure more in to do it again.

Whitney walked down to the sand and found Trudy sitting on the side watching it all happen, trying to hide the expression of horror on her face. Dead mer didn't seem to be her thing, and Whitney smiled at her friend to try to distract her. She was going to see a lot more death before the war was over, and that made her feel bad. In the night human world, Whitney was raised in, dead night humans happened, but the mer were isolated and the siren more so. What

Whitney didn't want to tell her it was that it was very likely Trudy was going to see people she loved dead by the time the whole thing was done, and quite possibly everyone she loved if they didn't find help in the Selkie.

"So this is going to work?" Whitney asked her friend; more than a little worried that Trudy wouldn't keep playing her part after seeing the results.

Trudy gave her a grim smile. "It's kill or be killed at this point, isn't it?"

And, unfortunately, it was. The other siren with her seemed to be having a hard time watching the dead mer being tossed into the fire, but they all seemed to share the same sentiment. They understood that even if they didn't like it, it was what it was.

"Yes. They are coming for the island and plan to kill every man, woman, and child on it. They don't want any siren surviving, so yes, it's kill them before they kill us. I know you all haven't seen much of this side of the night human world, but I can tell you, along with every hunter here, that this is the night human way. It sucks, and I'll do my best to make sure we get a future, but what you are doing now will help. Just remember that. Every little bit helps keep everyone back on the island safe. I went before the night human council to give us all a chance. Now we have to keep going to get that chance to live as free night humans." Whitney had to hope her speech was inspirational enough. The siren were all watching her, and that alone helped lift their spirits.

"They can stay in the river until we clean up," Jade suggested. She had been standing beside Whitney while she was giving her speech.

At least there was one hunter who didn't have a heart of stone yet. Rommy looked up from where they had just tossed the last body into the fire. She didn't disagree with her daughter. Even the famed hunter could see that the siren with her were just kids. Maybe she even had a bit of a heart left, too ... then again, Whitney had watched her move and kill more mer than anyone else with them.

The siren all made their way to the water to sit with their backs to the hunters. A few didn't look as comfortable turning their backs on an enemy who they had been drilled to hide from their whole lives, but they trusted Whitney, and she didn't hesitate to turn away from the hunters. Not watching it was probably the best solution, and sitting in the river would be safe.

"So while I'm gone, I'm leaving Trudy in charge. In reality, I'm still in charge and can hear any one of you if you need me. My fin makes you part of my clan now."

They all nodded like that was normal. It was far from normal for Whitney, but she was just going to go with it.

"I hope it won't take more than a day to go and bargain with them, but I have no idea what the Selkie will think of my offer. It might take some begging on my part, but that isn't beneath me at this point. I'll do everything I can to make sure we survive, and please do the same here."

Whitney looked into the face of each of the siren-Oceanids she was leaving behind. They were all scared, but at the same time, she could see determination behind the apprehension. They knew what was going on and what needed to be done. The moment she had pulled them from school, they all had to instantly grow up. It was time to protect each other and the siren who were back on the island that couldn't do so themselves. Whitney smiled at them. She might have been given a group of seven young greens, but now they were much more than that. She nodded to them and slipped into the stream.

"Don't do anything heroic ... rely on the hunters. They are trained to take out the mer and are here willingly. Let them handle the fighting, and you guys handle the luring of the mer to the river. Please stay safe."

Every face was looking at her and nodded back.

Whitney had to leave. She wanted more than anything to

stay around to keep them safe, but she knew her best shot at helping now was to talk to the Selkie.

**Whitney splashed her** tail a little quicker, picking up her pace at the same time. She didn't know it was possible for mer to get cold, but she was feeling the chill of the icy water. It wasn't unbearable, and she doubted it would kill her, but she was missing her warm Caribbean water. And she missed the warm sun. The gloomy skies above when she broke the surface were more than a little depressing. She didn't need depressing. She needed hope, and that was what she was searching for.

Sam had explained how to get to the Selkie Island.

*'Remember their leader is Mace. He's new and going to have to prove himself to everyone. He's about thirty or so and already has a family. If you're going to use the whole 'save them from the night human hunters if you join our new merworld,' then use your new status as a hook for his family,'* Sam told her quickly. Even he knew she was getting close, and he was going to have to break off contact. She couldn't afford any distractions.

*'I've got this, babe,'* Whitney said back more than a bit cheekily. Sam was worried. She didn't need to worry an ounce herself. He was doing enough for the both of them.

*'I'm not worried,'* Sam countered, picking up on her thoughts. *'I'm terrified that I won't see you again.'*

*'And you're jealous,'* Whitney added for good measure to distract him. She was always worried she wouldn't see him again. She was outside the siren island with no way home. She had faced the night human council and actually thought they were going to rule against her. Yes, he had thought the exact same thoughts, too.

*'Of course, I'm jealous. You are off putting your neck on the line time and time again for the siren, and I'm just sitting here in my father's office, while you're in danger- and Nic is*

*still sitting on the bottom of the ocean slowly bleeding out. I feel completely helpless. I wish I had the power to do more,'* he complained.

*'And you are. Go talk to Ken about Oceanids, and get the whole background on what he knows. There might be something more we can do with our new mer forms that we don't know about,'* Whitney added. She was getting close enough to see the blur of the barrier around the Selkie Island. *'I love you.'*

*'And I love you, too,'* Sam added before Whitney put up a wall between them.

It was time to see if she could convince a whole clan of mer to join a war. Whitney slowed down, waiting for some sort of invitation. She was sure they knew she was there. And her wait didn't take long thankfully, since she was still a bit cold. Eight brown-tailed mer swam up to her, all but one with weapons in hand. The last one was a girl, and she held a cloth in her hand. She motioned that she was going to tie it on Whitney's face. Whitney motioned for her to do so and was surprised in that it was tied around her mouth, not her eyes. Whitney didn't complain and followed the girl as she led the whole group past the barrier, to the island of ice waiting on the other side.

Two of the men hopped out and then helped the girl out of the water. Whitney pulled herself up to be seated on the ice ledge. The island wasn't an actual land mass like Whitney had expected. It was more of an ice island, or an iceberg of some sort. Whitney sat on the edge of the ice and felt the cold penetrate to her bones. She wasn't made for the temperature it was. Then again, from Sam's directions and never passing land, she very well could have been in the North Pole for all she knew. She was never one to run around freezing weather in basically a swimsuit and was not about to change on that one. She was freezing, and her breath puffed out clouds that looked like smoke. It was way too cold for her.

The others with her hopped out of the water and changed into their non-mer forms, all of which include heavy fur coats. A guy who was waiting too far away for Whitney to see clearly began walking toward her. He had on leather pants and large fur boots, but unlike the others in their coats, he only wore a fur vest that showed off his large biceps. His long, pulled-back hair accentuated his rough look. Only one person would walk around with such a presence in a night human camp. Whitney didn't need to ask who Mr. Tough Guy was. She already knew; this guy had to be Mace, the leader of the Selkie.

"Mmm mmm mmm," she said into the cloth.

The large man with dark, slicked-back hair finally made it to her. He eyed her over suspiciously. Whitney made no move to rise, though all the people that met her were now standing around watching her where she sat, almost as if waiting for her to attack. She wasn't going anywhere farther out of the water. At this air temperature, the water at least seemed warm now.

The leader leaned down and untied the cloth from her mouth. Whitney sat and stared at him. He didn't seem to have a problem with her voice.

"Obviously my people didn't look to see you have a pink tail." He offered her his hand to stand, but Whitney remained seated.

"But, sir, we had reports that Sam's mate had a pink tail," one of the men that had escorted her to the ice island stated. "She has a pink tail."

In a lightning quick movement, the man still holding her hand had turned and stared at the person speaking. Mace was staring daggers at the man, like he needed permission to talk, and as silent as the man now was, maybe he did need permission.

Trying her best to diffuse the hot situation, Whitney spoke, "I was trying to say before that I could stand, but since I'm in shorts and a tank top, I'd rather stay in the water."

Mace looked back at her, seeming to forget or ignoring the interruption. He held up a hand and snapped. One of the men took off his warm coat and handed it over to Mace without a word.

"I can't take your coat," Whitney said as Mace held it down to her.

Mace waved his hand, and the man walked away. "He'll be fine. We're used to this cold and really don't have to wear coats. We do it out of habit." Which would explain why he wore only a vest with nothing underneath it, Whitney thought.

Being sure that the guy wasn't standing there farther away, freezing in the cold, Whitney was relieved to see he was gone now. She didn't catch where he went, but that was enough to give herself permission to take his coat. Changing into her human legs, she stood up in her summer clothes and accepted the coat gratefully. It was still warm.

"I believe you must be here to talk, and I have a guess that Sam sent you," Mace said as he offered Whitney his arm.

Whitney took it and let the large man lead her back the way he came. When she went to ask how he knew she was from Sam, Mace grinned and answered before she could ask.

"I was on the beach when you made us all stop the battle. I was having so much fun, and normally I would have been angry at having to stop, but really, to feel that strength of command was just as exhilarating. It has been years since I've felt that kind of power. The old king didn't realize it was you, but man, when he finally figures it out, please take a picture of his face. I'd love a poster-sized print of it."

It appeared the Selkie didn't like the king of the siren that much either. And it seemed like Sam's knowledge of the Selkie leader was a bit limited, also. Maybe the Selkie leader wasn't as young as everyone thought. Whitney was a little scared it was going to be a failed mission before she stood a chance.

"So," Mace added as he turned and walked straight at what looked like a snow bank. Whitney prepared to turn again, but Mace marched right into the waiting snow. Whitney didn't mean to pull away, but he had expected her reaction and held tight to the hand she had on his elbow. Surprisingly, he pulled her right into the room with him that was hidden by the snow.

"I believe this should be more to your liking," he explained as they walked into what seemed like a large ice room, but there was a roaring fire going in the middle of the room and a large pool on the opposite side. At least two dozen Selkie were in the water, and all turned to watch them as they entered. Mace led her over near the pool of onlookers and stopped to offer her a chair that faced a rather larger chair, likely his throne, made up of animal bones and furs.

Whitney sat down and realized that the chair she was sitting in was fur-lined, too, and very warm. While she wasn't a vegetarian, all the furs around the room made her a little uneasy. At one point in her life, she used to be a furry animal, and everyone she loved had been one, too. At least they were all on the other side of the continent, and it wasn't likely that any of these furs were from animals she could have known. At least she hoped not.

"So, my pink-tailed mermaid, you've come here to speak to us. I presume it's about the war coming to the siren?"

"For one, yes," Whitney replied, putting on her game face. This was her part to play, and she was going to do it well. "But that's only part of it."

Mace raised an eyebrow. All the chit-chatting amongst the swimming Selkie stopped the moment they started talking. The room was silent, and her voice was the only thing in the room making a sound, as Mace didn't even talk.

"So first off, I am Sam's mate," Whitney said, getting that out in the open. It seemed like Mace already knew, but she didn't want anyone there thinking she was keeping that a secret. Little whispers began again. People were afraid that she was going to make them do something. Mace nodded to her. "But I'm not a siren."

Now the noise grew loud enough that Mace grumbled a bit in response. He turned his glare to the chattering Selkie, and they all stopped. It seemed he liked it more when it was silent. Whitney wasn't sure she wanted to know what sort of clan he ran. His people all seemed to fear him. He turned back to her with a pleasant smile. Okay, maybe he was a little manic or had multiple personalities.

"I'm intrigued. If you are Sam's mate—and from what I heard he created you—how can you not be a siren?"

"Well, I'm pretty sure you saw my tail. I'm not blue or green."

"Which I assumed made you a higher order of siren that they kept locked away," Mace concluded. That actually made sense and wasn't a theory she had thought of herself. He might have been a scary leader who with one glare could silence his people, but he was smart, also. Maybe there would be a way to reason with him.

"I had no idea what the tail meant until I went before and met the leader of the night human council only days ago." As expected, her words brought the audience in the pool back into their whispers. Now they didn't fear her, but thought she was crazy. No mer willingly went to the night human council.

"You went to the council?" Mace was completely intrigued.

"I went before the council to ask for a pardon for the siren. I went because I had nothing to do with the night human wars, and there's an island filled with siren who had nothing to do with them either. I willingly went to the council to try to get them to understand there are innocent mer in the ocean."

"And you are here now, so I am to assume they agreed with you?" Mace was quick on that one. It was nice that she didn't have to explain every detail because every time she talked, the Selkie were up in arms, but when he spoke, they grew silent again.

"They did. But they didn't give the entire siren clan a pardon. They gave me and my clan a pardon." Whitney let the people sitting around talk more. She needed them to believe her and the more they talked, the more she heard people say that what she was saying made sense. A pink tail wasn't a siren. Everyone knew that. And it seemed only Mace had seen her command the people to stop fighting weeks ago.

"Now I'm intrigued. I know just about every clan in every ocean. I have never come across a pink tail before. What clan do you belong to?" Mace stood and pressed his fingers together like he was racking his brain for the answer she was about to give. The whole room grew silent as they waited.

Whitney gave a shrug as he thought and let it all sink in for everyone there. If their leader couldn't come up with what she was, that was going to work in her favor. No one could dispute what she was going to tell them.

"Turns out, when Sam made me, he didn't make another siren because mer can't make new ones. Fate decided to make me into something that hasn't been around in a long time, but is needed now."

Mace's eyes grew large. He had figured out what she was saying. He obviously had studied the mer and knew this to be true, along with what she was going to add for everyone else who wasn't putting two and two together.

"I'm an Oceanid."


**It took over** an hour for Mace to get his people to calm down. The people in the pool seemed connected to others outside the large room they were in. As the news spread, others quickly began to file in. What went from a few dozen chattering at the prospect of a legendary mer in their presence became over a hundred or more packing tightly into the room. Whitney sat cozy in the warm furs and waited. She had a feeling that Mace would be swayed easier if more of his people were around to find out what she offered. While it seemed they would never disobey him, she needed them to want to be there, too. It wasn't just Mace she had to convince to help fight, but all the Selkie.

While people piled in and had to be updated by the people who were now out of the pool, Whitney just sat and watched. Mace seemed to do the same. He understood that more were coming, and he didn't need to rush it. Soon enough someone was offering Whitney drinks and food while she waited. Whitney had a small bite to eat, but her stomach was in knots because she still had more to say.

When the food was gone, and more people were arriving, she stood up and walked to the pool. The song of the cold water was different than her Caribbean. Whitney dipped her hand in as she waited and found the water much warmer than the outside sea water.

"Missing your mate?" Mace asked as he sat down beside her.

Whitney shrugged. Yes, the water made her think of Sam, but everything made her think of Sam. He was still on the island and busy, it seemed. She wanted to be back beside him, but it looked like her job in the coming war was on the other side from him.

"New mates need to be around each other," Mace said as he watched more people push into the large room. It seemed like a very large space until it was filled. Now there was barely any standing room left.

"I've heard that, but what can you do? I was the only one who could leave the island since I'm not a siren." Whitney shrugged again. There wasn't much she could do. And the draw of Sam was always worse when she thought about him.

"We are almost all here," Mace said as a couple more

people entered. "Then we can get back to our conversation." Mace stood and nodded to Whitney as he walked away. She doubted there was room for anyone else to get into the room.

Whitney stood up and walked back to her chair of honor, which was still empty. Mace wasn't in his seat, but she had to guess it wouldn't be official without him sitting in his kingly chair.

Mace stood in front of his chair and stared around the room.

"As everyone has been talking, let me introduce you all to the mer Whitney. She has traveled a long way to get to us, and thus we need to listen to what she has to say. No one will interrupt her or speak unless I give you permission. I've called everyone here because what she has to say involves us all."

Mace sat down in his chair and peered across at Whitney. There was no way he could read her mind, so why did he know what she had to say? Or was he just guessing? Whitney stood up and looked around the room. She could either face Mace or the people gathered. Not knowing which was less offensive, Whitney moved a few feet off to the side, turning to partially face Mace and partially face the Selkie.

"I've traveled from the siren island to ask for your help. I know that only a month ago, my mate, Sam, asked for help, and you came to his aid. I'm asking for help again. The siren are surrounded by thousands of mer soldiers. The island full of innocent people—women and children included—are waiting for the clans that have gathered to attack. Almost every clan has joined with the Lara, Undine, and Mavkas to try to destroy the siren. From what I gather, you guys don't exactly like the siren, but your hate isn't enough to warrant joining in on slaughtering them."

So far everyone seemed to agree with what she said. There was actually more dislike than she wanted to see, but she had a chance to change that.

"I've spoken with your leader to explain that while I'm a

mate to a siren, I'm not a siren. I technically don't have to go back and fight to help those people. I don't have to put myself in harm's way because I don't answer to the siren king. I'm an Oceanid."

Surprise should have laced everyone's face, but the ones that had been around before, and those who had been told about it already, were more curious than shocked. Now that she got that out of the way, she needed to lure them in.

"I've gone before the night human council to get a pardon for the siren mer, and I've been allowed to start my own clan of mer that will not be hunted on land by the hunters. My clan of mer will be safe and allowed access to the blood banks just like any other night human. This will be a completely new clan of mer, and a free clan. I don't want to rule over a clan. I hope to keep everything as it is as much as I can, with each kind of mer still living in their own communities. The only catch is that only those that are true of heart and not evil can join my clan, but I hope that the leaders I find in each mer clan will stay and rule over each individual clan." Whitney waited to see if Mace approved. He seemed intrigued by the idea, so she continued.

"Anyone who joins my clan will be free. I'm offering a place in this new mer world to anyone that helps the siren. I went before the night human council because I've met the siren. I know they are as innocent as I am. I truly believe they need a chance to be free in the night human world, and now they might all die. I ask for help in this war, and in exchange, you get freedom in the night human world as part of my new world of mer."

Whitney moved back over to her seat and sat down. That was all she could do, and she hoped it was good enough to sway at least some of them.

Mace stared at her like he was trying to figure her out. She had one angle, and that was to get them to help in the war. There was nothing else she wanted, and no matter how hard he looked at her, he was not going to find an ulterior motive. Not a single person in the room said a word as they waited to see what their king was going to decide. Finally, Mace nodded, and a woman stepped forward with a small girl in front of her. The child couldn't be more than five or six years old.

"Prove to us that you can change someone into an Oceanid, and we will then take a vote on whether to help or not."

Whitney nodded. That was an easy enough expectation. Whitney changed into her mer form and took a scale from her fin. Changing back, she motioned for the woman to come forward. Instead, she pushed the child forward. Whitney looked at Mace and could see in his eyes exactly who the child was. This was his daughter. If the whole clan decided to not go with her, at least his child would be free. It was a good call.

"Can I have your right arm?" Whitney asked the girl. She glanced back over her shoulder to her mother. Her mother nodded, and the child held out her arm. Pushing back her sleeve, Whitney pressed her scale to her forearm. The scale melted into her skin, leaving a pink circle in its wake. The girl stared at the mark.

"Now what?" Mace asked.

"Nothing. She's free in the night human world." It really was that easy. "The hunters are not to touch any mer with that mark. That means they are an Oceanid."

Mace studied the child. Standing up, he moved closer and stared at the small mark. Leaning in close, he scooped her into his arms as she transformed. Light brown fur covered her tail like all the other Selkie Whitney had seen, but now her upper body had the purple swirls from Whitney. While the Selkie tail was higher than the siren tail at the waist, the swirls still went around the child's neck and arms. She was still a Selkie, but also an Oceanid.

The Selkie, along with Mace, seemed to be transfixed by the difference in the child. No one said a word as he stood and held her above him for all to see. Whitney had to hope it would be enough to get people on her side... because they needed them. Heck, she needed more than just the Selkie, and she had to wonder if there were more in the other clans that wouldn't support war if they knew there was a different option. But how could she talk to everyone? War was coming quickly to the island, and she most likely didn't have time to swim all over convincing people to join her.

"And Whitney has proven what she can do," Mace finally told the shocked crowd. "While no one has seen an Oceanid in over a hundred years, I don't doubt what she is. Each and every one of you needs to take time and think of your choice. Will you join with her to save the siren and earn your own freedom, or will we wait out the war as we previously voted? Take thirty minutes to go home and discuss this with your family, then meet back here for the vote."

People all around them nodded before disappearing more quietly and quickly than they had arrived. Soon the place was empty except for the small girl and her mom who also remained behind.

"No matter what they decide, I'll be beside you in your fight," Mace told her once the room was empty. "You have given my daughter something I could never give her. She can grow up without the fear of being hunted. I owe you everything."

Whitney smiled faintly and nodded. One person wasn't going to make a difference, but she appreciated that he believed in her. If only he came back with her, it was going to be a suicide mission. Transforming again, Whitney took a second scale and offered it to his wife. The daughter shouldn't have to face her life alone.

Mace understood and took the scale to press into his wife's arm. They would both be free no matter what happened when the Selkie returned.

Whitney smiled while the lady was shocked into her new role. She had tears pouring down her face as she couldn't say a word. It didn't take anything more than that for Whitney to realize this was her purpose in the mer world. They had broken down into clans that hated each other. It was time to bring them back together. She could do that. She *would* do that, if she made it out of the war alive.

"Thank you," the little girl said as her mother was still in shock that she was now free to live in the human world. "Purple is my favorite color." She gave Whitney her biggest grin. The child had no idea what the change meant, but was still thanking her.

Whitney didn't need thanks. She needed to win the war and save the mer that deserved to be free.

There was little time left. She understood the whole waiting around to decide what the Selkie were doing, but she was needed back at the island. They needed to plan more. Sitting and waiting really wasn't the best option.

"I need to leave," Whitney said. She hated to leave before they had decided, but she had spent too much time sitting already.

Mace nodded. At least he understood the urgency.

"Once you decide what to do, have your wife contact me. Like the bond between the clans and their leader, I'm bound to the Oceanids. All she has to do is call to me, and I can hear her."

Mace nodded again. "Thank you."

Whitney shook his outstretched hand before making her way out of the building and back to the ocean. As she reached the edge of the ice, she took off the coat and boots she had borrowed and left them folded up on the ice before she dove into the sea in her mer form. There might have been people on the side watching, but she didn't notice or turn back. She had a job to do, and it was time to get the war over. She had another task to accomplish, the real reason why she was in the mer world.

## CHAPTER 8

**Sam was shocked** that Whitney had done it. He had his doubts as he sent her off to ask them, but the Selkie were now going to help. The Selkie were fierce fighters and were more than enough to keep the battle even-sided. He just didn't think they would join after the last battle. The new Selkie leader had owed Sam a favor and was obligated to come, but now he was actually coming on his own terms. Even better, all the Selkie fighters were coming. Sam shouldn't have doubted her. If anyone could convince someone to do something, it was Whitney.

Sam wanted to take time to relax and celebrate Whitney's achievement, but now he was busy with his brother, Ken, who had come up with a way to detect the traps and was currently testing it out. Once he was certain it would work, Sam planned to go get Nic. His other older brother wasn't going to survive much longer with the blood he was losing, and with everything coming they needed to get him soon. Sam trusted Ken would figure it out perfectly.

"How much longer?" Sam asked as Ken surfaced with a face full of navy blue ink. Ken's plan used the ink from squids and something else Sam didn't understand, and didn't care to understand. Ken was certain he could figure it out, and that was enough.

"I don't know," Ken replied, wiping the ink off his face but leaving a smear in its wake.

Sam huffed a little but didn't yell at his brother. At least Ken was doing something. Their father had written Nic off as another dead son already. Sam wasn't sure how the old man could be so callous. He didn't seem to care when any of his other sons died, and now it was the same for Nic. He had sons to spare, but that shouldn't matter. They were his children. The man had to be soulless. And that made Sam worry just a tad.

Whitney had explained that becoming an Oceanid meant you had to be "good" as she put it. What he figured it meant was that you had to have a soul, and if his father didn't, he was sure his mother would be trapped by the man, being the last of the siren. Sam still wasn't at the point of caring for the old man, but he did care what happened to his mother.

"I need to make some adjustments and try it again," Ken told him.

Reaching down, Sam handed him another squid. "We need him back," he emphasized.

Nic was in charge of the guards. It wasn't just that Sam wanted him back; they had to have him back. Nic knew more about the protection of the island than anyone besides Sam. Sam didn't want to lead the battle again the mer alone. He needed Nic beside him.

*'And what about me?'* Whitney asked in his mind.

Sam smiled. She had been eavesdropping again. He found now that she was an Oceanid, it seemed to come more natural for her to tap into his mind. And it seemed she created a stronger barrier than he did as he had tried on several attempts to see how it was going with the Selkie, and he failed each time. He knew her song was stronger than his, but now everything seemed to be growing stronger for her. A little unfair, but so far his ego was able to handle it.

*'I want you somewhere safe,'* Sam replied. And that was the truth. He wanted her nowhere near the battle that was coming. He wanted her locked away in a safe box where he didn't have to worry about her getting hurt.

*'And I want you safe, too, you know.'*

Sam chuckled. Oh, he knew that. He had a feeling all her looking into his mind was to make sure he was staying safe. While he had been tempted more than once to just charge the waiting mer to go and find her, he had more control than that. At least that was what he was telling himself over and over again. So far that had worked.

*'I think the safest place for us both is to be together,'* Whitney added.

How could he deny that? He was going stir-crazy with worry about her and having nowhere to go since he was stuck on the island. A steel box to keep her safe was still ideal, but second was having her beside him where he could at least see what sort of trouble she was getting into.

*'Trouble?'* she asked innocently.

*'Yes, because you haven't made my heart skip a beat at least twice a day now since you left me,'* Sam replied. And that was an understatement. It was more like he was worrying constantly about her. She was running into trouble every time Sam talked to her.

*'Ha, ha, ha,'* she replied, though she had to know it was true. Their connection was much stronger now, and he knew she was fake laughing. There was very little he didn't feel from her; it had to be the same way for her. *'I'm almost back to the island, and then I have a plan. I'll see you soon,'* she told him.

Sam wanted to pry deeper into her plan, but she was too good at keeping it all locked away. He was going to have to wait until she checked in with him again. And that was fine. He had his own stuff to deal with ... mainly getting Nic out of the sea and healing him. They needed him back in action, and hopefully, Ken was going to get it right this time so Sam could go save their brother. With Whitney busy, she was unlikely to know what he was up to and stop him before he could do it. Ken would make it as safe as possible, but there was always the chance Sam might get hurt. He was more than happy to leave that conversation until later.

**Whitney made it** back to the island in time to see them hauling away their latest kill. The fire was still roaring even though it was morning and the sun was warm enough to not need a fire for heat. Whitney climbed up onto the shore and made her way into the trees. Most of the siren were behind the fire, tucked away by the river, sleeping.

"Good trip?" Jade asked as she walked up to Whitney while wiping her hands on her bloodstained pants.

"Yes, and here, too, I see?"

"Mom keeps count, but I think we've taken care of probably one hundred or so mer."

Whitney calculated that out in her head. Being able to talk to the Selkie on her swim back gave her more details. Mace told her there were over fifteen hundred fighting mer in the waters with at least a thousand more as back-up waiting to be sent. Even killing one hundred at a time, it was going to take them weeks to get rid of all the mer. They didn't have the supplies or the energy to fight for weeks. In reality, everyone needed to be on the island getting ready for the big battle that was coming. Whitney had a plan to do just that.

"Do you still have my phone?" Whitney asked. She had left it behind on the island because she wasn't sure where she was going to end up. Why carry a phone with her to worry about if she was going to be countries away from her cell coverage anyway?

"Yes, but no phones work this far out in the ocean," Jade replied, digging in her pocket and handing it over.

"No phones that aren't magically enhanced by a witch," Whitney replied with a wiggle of her eyebrows.

"You know a witch?" Jade asked in awe.

Whitney nodded.

"So unfair. You could have told me that before. Witches come in handy when you fight certain night humans. You have to hook me up," Jade added as Whitney turned on her phone.

There was still plenty of battery left, and she was glad to find that without having to go back to shore to charge it. She was going to have to thank Cassie yet again for putting the spell on her phone, but she was planning to do that in person. Whitney dialed her friend's number and waited as it rang.

"Cas?" Whitney asked as someone picked up on the other end of the line.

"Whit?" a male voice asked in return.

Whitney's eyes bugged at the voice. It had been months since she had talked to her other best friend.

"Owen?" she squealed, making Jade jump. 'Sorry,' she mouthed to Jade as the other hunters turned to them and gave them questioning looks. Whitney knew how much Jade hated being the center of attention.

"Fine, fine, fine," Owen said on the other end of the line. "I just wanted to say hi and how cool it is that she's a night human again." Obviously, he wasn't talking to Whitney.

Owen, Cassie, and Whitney were best friends until she moved away. They hung out all the time and did almost everything together. Owen was like the older brother she always wanted, and he loved her like his own little sister. It had been just as hard on him as it had been on Cassie since Whitney had moved away. Probably harder for him because Cassie at least had her mate, Nate, to turn to now. Owen lost both his friends in one night, and he wasn't mated yet.

"Her Highness declares I must hand over the phone to her before she goes all evil witch on me and turns me into a toad," Owen joked.

Whitney smiled. It was great to hear his voice and fairytale references again. The boy was one odd combination of good looks and a weird sense of humor that kept most people away. This was probably why he ended up with Cassie and Whitney, the two outcasts in their last school.

"It was great to hear your voice," Whitney quickly said, since she knew Cassie wasn't going to be patient and turning him into a toad probably wasn't just a threat. Cassie could do much more than just turn someone into a frog on command.

"You, too. You have to come visit soon. It's boring here

without you."

"Boring?" Cassie exclaimed from behind him. "I'll make sure to tell Michelle you called her boring." The phone dropped with a clank.

"You wouldn't," Owen replied, now farther away from the phone.

"Thanks for my phone back," she yelled, probably because Owen was running away from her. "Hey, Whitney. How's the whole war thing going?"

"I need another favor," Whitney told her, getting right to the point. "I have to get everyone back to the island. Well, technically I need to get back to the island, but I figured it would be best if I brought everyone with me. If I send you a picture of a tree, can you come and transport us? I know how to get us to the island without having a picture." That was their last hang-up about going directly to the island before.

Jade now stared at Whitney. She didn't appear eager to go to the siren island. Regular humans were far from welcome in any night human home, let alone hunters. Whitney grinned back at her.

"Yes. Send it over, and I'll be right there," Cassie replied before hanging up.

That was the first step. Get everyone to the island and rested, because they were going to need to be full of energy when the battle really started.

"Hey, I survived going over to your house with your mother around, you should be fine coming to my island." Whitney winked at her. "I will promise I won't snack on you, but I can't say the same for all the guys back there. Mister Bouncer Guy might have some competition to catch you."

Jade tried not to smile at Whitney's joking. It was true. Whitney had been to the hunter house when she was an illegal night human, and she was very lucky they didn't know and kill her on the spot. It wasn't quite the same to bring the hunters to the island now, but they needed to be back there to help with their planning. The Selkie were coming from the water, and Whitney wanted the hunters on land to protect the Selkie from the hunters. They wouldn't know how to tell the difference if they came across one otherwise.

"If I leave you here it's going to take a few weeks of killing like you've done all night to get rid of the mer. We don't have enough supplies here on the island, nor do we have the time. And probably after a while, someone will catch on. We need to get back to the siren island to help out and make a plan to win this thing."

"It went that well?" Jax asked as he came up to them.

Whitney took a picture of the tree next to them. She sent the message to Cassie before looking up at Jax.

"It seems that I offer something better than the other clans can. Glad to know my pink fin is good for something other than attracting attention from the siren for not being blue or green." Whitney had explained some of the siren world to her friends, and she made sure to put in there the whole hierarchy crap she had been dealing with.

Cassie stepped out of the tree beside them. Of course, her bodyguard cat was with her.

"So move everyone to the island?" Cassie asked, holding her hand out for another picture.

"First, just me. I want to be sure no one attacks without thinking if I bring a bunch of hunters on the island," Whitney explained, not handing her the phone. "And I don't have a picture from the island. Technology doesn't work there."

Cassie gave her a confused look, obviously wondering how she was supposed to get them to the island since her magic didn't include walking on water.

"Yeah, I know ... confusing," Whitney quickly added. "On my swim back here I got thinking about how you can only go to places you've seen before. That made me wonder how to get back to the island since I don't have any photos of the place. As I thought more about how you just pull through a tree, I began to realize the whole reason you can do that is because you're a night human. Since that's the case, then I should be able to just share a memory with you with a blood connection."

The simplicity of it dawned on Cassie's face, and she laughed.

"You know, I have to make things so complicated, I never thought of that," Cassie admitted.

Whitney nodded. It had taken hours of swimming in the ocean alone for Whitney to think of it, so she didn't blame her. She didn't completely see Cassie as a night human anyways, and she doubted she ever would. Cassie had been a day human her whole life and was raised as a day human. There was just too much day human in her.

Whitney held out her hand and took the knife Jade offered her. Slicing her fingertip, she handed the blade to Cassie, who did the same. As they pressed their fingers together, Whitney felt the instant connection. Even if she wasn't holding her hand, she would know this was her friend's presence. Everything about it said Cassie.

*'Here's the tree near my home,'* Whitney explained, thinking of the great big tropical tree that had the best-smelling flowers on it. Cassie took a moment and let go of her hand.

"Well that was strange," Cassie commented.

*Strange?*

"It was like your whole world was pink-tinted, and here I just thought you liked the color pink. I think you might actually *be* the color pink."

Whitney stuck her tongue out at Cassie as Jax and Jade laughed. Everyone knew her love of the color pink, but they still found the need to tease her about it.

"Well, bestie, let's get you back on your island where you can introduce me to your hunky mate. I think I caught a glimpse of him in your mind, but I have to see for myself to be sure."

Whitney turned back to her two hunter friends.

"Can you keep everyone safe as they sleep?"

"Got it, boss," Jax teased as Jade nodded.

"Time to go home," Cassie said to her as she waited by the tree with her hand outstretched for Whitney.

Strangely, it was going to work. All it took was having a few free hours to think, and Whitney had found a way back to the island and Sam. He was going to be surprised. Cassie wiggled her eyebrows as she waited. She had her own mate, so it didn't bother Whitney at all that she called him hunky. Actually, all his screaming fans at his rock concerts thought the same thing, and that didn't bother her either because hunky Sam was hers.

**Whitney stepped forward** to the house even though she knew Sam wasn't there. Cassie waited tentatively by the tree, taking in the whole island from their front step. It was a spectacular view. Sam wanted to be away from everything, so his house was kind of up a hill and was the last one on the path. Everything stretched out before where they stood and they could even see all the way down to the ocean.

"You didn't tell me you lived in paradise," Cassie commented as her panther sat down. He was enjoying the view, too.

"That depends on how you describe paradise. Personally, I love it here, but Sam's not the biggest fan of the island. It's too isolated for him. Truthfully, though, I don't know how I'd feel about it if I couldn't get away from it for over a decade."

"There's always a downside to everything," Cassie replied, looking at the cat at her feet. Jared only had his night human cat, which he had yearned to be for years, back in the days before his human life was taken away and he became permanently stuck in that form.

"We need to go down into town to find Sam. I figured he'd be home, but it seems like he isn't," Whitney told her. It would have been easier to find Sam's mind and a tree next to him, but she wanted it to be a surprise. Now she just needed to follow the pull to him. He'd feel her coming, but he didn't expect her to be on the island, so it still could be a surprise.

Whitney led the way down the paths. She'd expected to get a lot of stares with a non-siren and panther walking with her, but now that they'd arrived, she found no one out and about. It was strangely quiet.

"It's not normally this empty. They must be busy," Whitney explained to her friend, though she was really just trying to reassure herself.

"An island preparing for war should be busy. I guess they don't plan to hide here in town if something happens, which is a smart choice," Cassie analyzed the situation.

As she traveled down another hill and around the bend, Whitney knew where the bond was leading her. Sam was somewhere near the amphitheater, and with the empty town, she wasn't too excited to surprise him now. Yes, surprising him sounded fun, but in front of hundreds of people, not so much. Whitney cautiously kept going toward Sam and only peeked into the amphitheater. No one was in the seats or on the stage. Sam was near, but he wasn't there.

"Siren are into theatre?" Cassie asked as followed Whitney down the stairs to the stage.

Whitney couldn't help it. She had to laugh. Thinking of the siren performing a musical number on the stage was actually quite funny.

"No, this is our central meeting place," Sam said as he came out from behind the stone wall of the stage.

Skipping the last few stairs, Whitney jumped onto the stage and ran over into his arms. Sam easily scooped her up and hugged her before setting her down to kiss her like he hadn't seen her in years. Whitney melted into his lips. Everyone was right—mates should never spend long times apart. Whitney only drew back when there was a cough behind her.

"So, Sam, this is Cassie. Cassie, this is Sam," Whitney introduced them with her cheeks flaming red. She really wasn't one for public displays of affection, but everything had changed with Sam. She didn't care who was watching. She needed that hug and kiss just as much as she now required blood to live.

"Pleased to finally meet the guy who's been keeping my best friend from me, and I'm glad I don't have to beat you up for making her into an outlawed night human since she took care of that now, too," Cassie replied. Then she gave him a nice smile.

Whitney wasn't sure if her friend really was mad at Sam or not, but her non-aggressive ways seemed threatening with a panther beside her.

"Oh, yeah, and this is Jared's cat," Whitney introduced the panther.

"The one that saved your life?" Sam asked. He walked forward and knelt down in front of the cat. "Thank you for your sacrifice. Whitney told me that you, along with Cassie and Nate, saved her from dying. I can never thank the three of you enough. Without you guys, I would have never had a mate."

Now Cassie appeared taken aback by Sam's honesty. He was truly grateful for the skinwalkers, and not mad at her hostility toward him. And what he said was more than true. They had saved Whitney, and he had planned to never take a mate until he met her.

"I came to find you and ask if the siren and hunters can all come back to the island," Whitney explained, getting back on track. Before Sam could answer, she added, "They have killed over one hundred mer thus far. They're on our side and will be safe around us. The siren are pardoned."

Sam nodded, but didn't reply. He briefly closed his eyes, and then looked back at her. It was one of the quickest conversations she had ever seen him have with his father.

"I think my dad is actually scared of what's to come. He said yes, but we have to keep them at our place," Sam replied.

"That's the house we first came to," Whitney told Cassie, who nodded.

"I'll bring them right away." Cassie jogged back up the stairs to find the closest tree without having to be told. That's what best friends were like, and especially Cassie with Whitney. It was as if they could finish each other's thoughts almost all of the time, and even though they had been apart months without any talking, it was still like that.

"So why are you hanging out here?" Whitney asked once Cassie was gone. She had thought he would be soaking at home. His father was driving him nuts, and everyone had a job to do but Sam lately.

Sam reached forward and took her hand, keeping her beside himself.

"We were able to get Nic back, but it's going to take a long time to heal him," Sam replied. "He lost most of his fin and lots of blood. We can't feed him until the wounds heal, and hopefully, the tail grows back."

Whitney could see the images in Sam's mind of what it was like to find his brother. He was almost eaten through by the trap, and freeing him actually brought sharks to the island due to the blood that was floating around. Not only did Sam have to get his beaten brother back to shore, but he had to do it with sharks nipping at him.

Sam led the way he had come, and Whitney found Nic lying in a bathtub-sized bucket of water. His fin was missing the lower half, and his eyes were closed, like he was sleeping. He didn't look much better than he had in Sam's mind.

"It's the healing water," Sam explained.

"Is he dead?" Whitney asked as she watched him. She couldn't tell if he was breathing.

"No. He's in a self-induced coma. He's keeping a block between him and his mate so that she doesn't have to suffer with him. He's been doing this since he got caught. She's doing fine and taking care of their kids. As long as he can keep the block up, she won't get hurt, too."

Whitney walked over and looked at Nic. He was in pain as he grimaced, but if he was keeping his connection to his mate shut, then he was doing what every male siren would do. He was protecting his loved ones.

"Where does the water come from?" Whitney asked. She had experienced the water once when Sam was flayed for saving her life. It was the reason the siren accepted her, when she realized now that they shouldn't have. She wasn't technically a siren.

"There's a fresh spring behind here that we get the water from," Sam replied with a raised eyebrow. He knew she was up to something.

"Do you have to keep changing it for Nic?"

"Yes ..." Sam still stared at her.

"Would there be enough to fill that glass ball thingy from before that I sat in?"

"Yes. It refills more often than we need it."

Sam still was confused, but Whitney wasn't. An idea had come to her, and she just might have the solution to keep the innocent mer safe. She didn't know why, but she knew it would work. It was her Oceanid senses kicking in again. Her plan was fail-proof. Now all she had to do was convince Sam.

## CHAPTER 9

**Sam stared at** Whitney from inside the glass bowl. It wasn't a position he ever wanted to be in. He was sitting helpless and couldn't do anything but watch. This wasn't how he was supposed to take care of his mer, or his mate. It was only months ago that she sat in this very glass bowl and had to watch him be fried. It would be easier to be the one being punished now than to sit and watch everything. He'd complain that it wasn't fair, but he knew better than to add that, because Whitney would say that was exactly how she felt when he went through it. But it still wasn't fair.

"I'm going to need hundreds of scales," Whitney told her four siren friends that were with her on the same block he once laid upon.

The king stood off to the side. He wasn't about to hurt her like he did his son. He knew now what she was and believed in her bringing luck as much as the night human Loan had, but instead of just good luck, the king thought his involvement would bring the siren bad luck. At least her greens weren't as superstitious, or they didn't think she was some legendary creature. Either way, they were going to help in her plans and Sam had basically no say.

Sam had already seen how she had changed her friends with just one scale. He, along with his family, had been amazed what it had done. The grotesque second-class greens looked normal when they transformed now. The pink scales of the Oceanid were mixed into their green scales now. Sam hadn't admitted to his family that he had also changed at the same time Whitney became a full Oceanid, but they would see soon enough. The only one who had seen his new mer form was currently unconscious.

"So if I just used the blade scraping backward, it should pull the scales off?" Whitney asked again, and the king nodded.

She had never skinned a fish before, and his father had on more than one occasion. Sam doubted she would be able to do it. He had seen his father punish by removing scales and it wasn't a pretty sight. It was going to be painful for both of them.

"And when I have to stop, you promise me you'll continue?" Whitney looked at one of the green guys that she was friends with. Sam knew their names, but right now he was still angry she was going through with her impossibly painful idea. He didn't mind pain, but he minded that she was going to take the brunt of it.

Whichever guy it was nodded.

*'You don't have to do it this way,'* Sam told her, knowing it would fall on deaf ears.

*'I need to make my people, and the sooner, the better. There could be innocent mer going into this war, and they don't know that they stand a chance of a new life if they don't fight at all. I have to give them the chance.'*

It was the same argument she had been using for the last hour. Sam still wasn't happy about it. He understood what she wanted to do and he understood that it was important, but why the heck did his mate have to suffer and feel the pain she was about to go through? It wasn't fair. He would much rather be the one on the cutting board getting descaled.

Sam knew the determination in her eyes meant he didn't get a say in it. In reality, he understood that, too. She was making the choice, and she was choosing to harm herself. He would do his job and sit in the water to heal them both. That was as much as he could do at this point. She was more stubborn than she would ever admit. Even now she was blocking him out; otherwise, she would have scolded him for calling him stubborn. She was actually going to go through with her plan.

Whitney held the knife by her tail. Taking a few deep breaths, her hand didn't move at all, and she shook her head. Sam smiled. She didn't have it in her to hurt herself, and he didn't blame her. It was going to hurt ... and hurt a lot. He may have been to blame for putting that idea into her head, since his thoughts were constantly trickling into hers. He didn't care.

Whitney turned to her friends. The greens with her looked as queasy as she did. It seemed like Sam might get his way after all, but that wouldn't win them the war or make his mate happy. Whitney wanted to save the mer, and she needed her scales to do it. He'd much rather she picked one off at a time, but she wanted more than she could easily pick off. He knew she was right, but he was still happy she wasn't going to go through all the pain.

Whitney glanced up at her friends, and none of them moved. He could see her indecision. She hated to use her siren song to make her friends do anything, but it was going to have to come to that. He wasn't about to help. He liked her in one piece. They could find a different way, and he was willing to sit all night looking for one.

Whitney pleaded with her friends with her eyes. She needed their help, and the rest of the siren weren't about to give it. Sam hated that he won this battle, but he would look for different options, and if he had to sit and pick each scale off by hand, he would do that, too.

**Whitney stared at** her friends. They weren't moving. She had failed. She couldn't cut off her own scales because she was too afraid of how much it would hurt, and none of them could hurt her either. She should have expected that. They were her Oceanids now. There was probably something built in that made them unable to hurt her. She was asking too much of them.

When she looked over at the siren king, she knew there

would be no help there either. He was beyond superstitious about her new mer standing. He even went to bowing his head to her when she entered a room or talked now. It was more than a little strange. What she needed was someone she trusted to not kill her to scrape off her scales, but the island still wasn't completely home to her. The people she trusted fully were either skinwalkers or humans.

*'Go get Jax and Jade,'* Whitney told Trudy silently. Trudy's eyes bugged as she knew what Whitney wanted, and Sam was going to be mad. *'Don't worry about Sam. I don't trust anyone but you guys, Jax, and Jade. They won't harm me.'*

Trudy seemed to agree with that and hurried away.

*'Where's she going?'* Sam asked as he watched from his bubble.

*'To get me help. I'm doing this whether you approve or not. You can't come up with a better solution, and we both know it needs to happen now. Every little thing we can do to win this war needs to be done, and we don't have time to sit and pluck one scale off at a time. I'm not going down without a fight.'* Whitney was determined to save these mer, and this was her part to play.

Sam couldn't argue against that, and he was smart enough to not try to.

It took only minutes for Trudy to return with Jax and Jade. Her face was as red as her curls like she'd run the whole way there and back. Whitney smiled at her friend, who tentatively returned it.

"I know this is what you want, but I'm still kind of with Sam in wishing there was another option," Trudy told Whitney as Jax and Jade stood beside her on the stone slab she was lying on. Trudy was almost as much against the plan as Sam, but she knew what it felt like to go from a green to an Oceanid. She couldn't deny that for her family and friends who were green, and knew Whitney was right in what she wanted to do.

"Trudy didn't explain anything beyond you needed our help," Jade said as she gazed down at Whitney.

Whitney slipped her arms back into the metal chains attached to the slab; the same ones that held Sam down as his father poured hot coals over his fin months ago.

"Basically I need you to flay me ... well, not flay, but I need you to scrape the scales off my fin. I need to be able to change the mer into Oceanids before the battle starts. There might be some that are innocent and will want to live a free life instead of fighting. I need to try, and I need to mark the Selkie and Siren so that you guys know who not to attack."

Jax nodded and took the knife from Noah. The hunters were coming in handier than she had first expected.

"So I imagine this is going to hurt a lot?" Jax asked, picking up on the expressions of the people around them, and maybe even the glare coming from Sam.

Whitney nodded and tried not to show how nervous she was about all of it.

"And Sam in that fish bowl has something to do with it?"

Yes, he had caught the glare from Sam.

"Sam's in spring water that heals siren. When you cut me, it should transfer to him, and he should heal, which should transfer back to me." Whitney was letting the secret out as to how they fooled the siren before, but she didn't care now. She wasn't exactly a siren, so she didn't have to follow their rules anyway.

"Jade, hold her arms down," Jax told his sister. Jax reached down and flicked a scale, judging what he needed to do. They were pressed tightly to Whitney's tail, but they were loose. They weren't attached completely around all the edges. Jax nodded as he understood what needed to be done.

"Sam won't come after him for doing this?" Jade asked as she held Whitney's hands rather than holding down her arms.

"No, he won't," Whitney said, looking across the way at Sam. *'And you won't. I know you don't like hunters, but I asked them to do this, and you can't hold a grudge.'*

*'I can't hold a grudge against someone that came to help you when they didn't have to,'* Sam said, admitting defeat and referring to the fact that Jax and Jade came to the island when the hunter council hadn't sent them. *'By the way, does my dad know Rommy is here, too?'*

Whitney's eyes bugged. She hadn't thought about that. Rommy and the siren king seemed to have some sort of history which made them hate each other. Sam didn't know much about it, and neither did Jade or Jax. But there was definitely bad blood between them. Over the years they had tried to kill each other more than a dozen times, and neither could succeed. It probably wasn't the best idea to bring the hunter to the island, but they did need her help.

*'Oops, I guess I forgot to mention that detail,'* Whitney replied as she glanced over at Sam's dad. He was eyeing Jax and Jade like he recognized them, and he probably did even though he'd only met them once. *'Guess he knows now.'*

The king looked like he was ready to leave when Sam called to him.

"Father, we need you to stay here and make sure this goes okay. If Whitney loses too much blood, you need to put her in the spring water with me," Sam told his father. The old man seemed to debate and realized Sam was right. From inside the bubble, Sam couldn't transfer her into the water with him if it went bad. Sam might not have wanted Whitney to do what she planned, but he wasn't going to let her possibly get hurt further, either.

"Are we ready now?" Jax asked, locking eyes with Sam.

Sam nodded to him as the king stayed in his spot. Jax turned back to Whitney, and she nodded, too, squeezing Jade's hand before anything started.

"Look at me," Jade said as she stood over her friend's head.

Whitney gazed up into the hunter's eyes. She could see in the depths of them that her friend had endured and knew about pain.

"Can't be much worse than shaving with a dull razor, right?" Whitney joked. She didn't know what else to do. The pain she couldn't inflict on herself was coming as soon as Jax began.

Jade grimaced at the badly timed joke. "Focus just on me."

Whitney did just that as her fin felt like it was being burned. Grimacing and closing her eyes made it feel worse. More was coming off her. Whitney gritted her teeth to keep from screaming. She was sure with just one scream Sam would call the whole thing off. She needed to be strong. Looking back at Jade's eyes seemed to help. There was strength and compassion there waiting for her as more pain ripped through her. For what seemed like an eternity, Whitney stared at her friend—a siren and a hunter. An impossible match for a friendship. As she felt the last of her scales on the front of her fin be ripped away, Jade held her place over her with her eyes never leaving hers.

Jade was a friend for life. It seemed unimaginable, yet it worked. They had completely different upbringings, and came from completely different worlds, but there was something they shared. It was like Whitney found someone who was facing the same odds she was always facing—survive or be dead. And her friend was surviving and helping her survive.

"Can we get some of that healing water on her before I get the other side?" Jax asked, finally breaking Whitney's concentration from Jade.

Whitney felt the cold, soothing water rest on her fin. It still burned, but it wasn't as bad as it was when he had started. Actually, as he took more scales, it was like her tail had gone completely numb. If she didn't know better, she would have assumed shock. Then again, maybe it was.

Jax finally finished and stood up. He nodded to Jade, and Jade, in turn, nodded to Whitney. The torture session was done for the moment. Whitney took a deep breath to try to calm her beating heart. It was done for now.

Finally letting go of Jade's hands, Whitney pulled her arms from the chains and sat up to see the damage. Her beautiful tail was ragged with scales. Only a few had grown back, and bits remained of others. Another one popped through the surface of her tail skin and began to grow. Amazingly, growing scales actually hurt, too. Here she thought the only painful part of the process was getting the scales off.

*'It will hurt less as more come back,'* Sam explained.

Whitney nodded to him and finally saw that inside his bowl a few of his own blue scales were floating around. As her scales were ripped off, so were his. She felt more than a little guilty for that. She never in her life wanted to cause him pain, but she had.

*'Never,'* Sam scolded her. *'I had you burned alive. Don't feel guilty about a few scales coming off. I barely felt it.'*

"How long before she's back to normal?" Jade asked, turning to the siren king. She knew who he was.

The king shrugged. "We punish with burning coals, so I'm not sure how long it will take."

Jade nodded and looked at her brother.

Jax held up the bucket the green had collected the scales into. "Will this be enough?" Jax asked, holding it up for Whitney to see inside.

The bucket was more than half full. She wasn't really sure if it would be enough. It wasn't like she had time to count it, or even count how many people she might need to change. She was more than ready to turn over and have him skin off the back side of her tail even knowing how bad it would hurt. She was willing to do whatever it took to save the siren and her new Oceanids.

"It has to be enough because I won't let her do that again," Sam said from his bowl.

Jax got the hint and nodded to the slightly angry siren.

Now Whitney just had to wait for her scales to grow back. The growing back part was slower than scraping them off. They were coming along great, and one by one it was looking closer to normal. Feeling each one poke through was quite itchy, and she kept her hands away from her fin in case it hurt to touch. As red and raw as it was, it looked likely that it would.

"So what do you do from here?" Jade asked, distracting her from watching the scales grow back and wincing as new ones poked through her delicate skin.

"We turn all the good guys into Oceanids, and I send them home. Well, I will give them the option to leave and hope they will just go home. I really don't know what they will do." Whitney had a lot of hopes, and she crossed her fingers that this would work.

The king waved his hand at Sam, and he was out of the water. Immediately transforming, he hurried over to Whitney's side. Gingerly, he touched her fin. It didn't hurt as much as she expected it to. Sam scooped her into his arms.

"We are heading home until you're fully healed. You can transform everyone later. Now you need to rest." Sam wasn't taking no for an answer, and Whitney didn't have much fight left in her. She needed to change the people soon and let them know they didn't have to fight, but she did need rest.

Jax and Jade turned to follow, but Sam stopped and motioned for them walk in front of him. Jax raised an eyebrow at Whitney, but she had no clue what it was about. Sam wasn't going to stab him in the back or anything, and she got the feeling from him he was protecting the hunters, not getting ready to get revenge on them. He turned back to his father.

"Rommy is here as an ally. You need to leave your differences alone and let her help us. She's worth at least half a dozen trained siren in this fight. You take her out, and we might lose because of it, so leave her alone."

Sam's argument must have been good enough because

the old king didn't get mad or respond at all. Sam nodded to Jax and Jade to keep walking, and Whitney laid her head on Sam's shoulder. He was correct, but she didn't want to tell him so that he could gloat. She was tired. Soon enough she found her eyes drooping and they weren't even back home yet. She didn't care. She was in Sam's arms and safe. The hard part was done—at least the painful part was done—and it was time to sleep.

**Whitney woke in** Sam's arms. She could hear the people in the house, but their bedroom was empty aside from them. It was nice, safe, and warm, and she almost didn't want to open her eyes to admit she was really awake. It would have been easier to just stay in her safe place and pretend the siren island wasn't going to be attacked. Sam's other arm snaked around her and pulled her closer. He knew she was awake and yet didn't say anything. He was pretty comfy in her safe place also.

A crash outside the bedroom made her lift up her head. Sam gently patted her back down to his chest.

"It seems that the great hunter Rommy doesn't do well with cooking and is a bit frustrated," Sam said, explaining the noise. He wasn't worried in the least.

Whitney kind of wanted to go peek and see what was going on. It was bound to be fun to watch, but then again, she wasn't sure she wanted to see an angry hunter. It was a hard choice.

"How do you feel?" Sam asked, running a hand down her head and tangling his fingers in her blonde curls.

"Better," Whitney replied. And she did feel better, but was still tired. It took a lot more energy to regrow her scales than she expected. "What did your dad think of your new tail?"

The old king never said anything out loud, but she was sure he scolded him mentally. Sam was still connected to his father, even if Whitney wasn't, and he hadn't told his father about the new Oceanid scales he was sporting now.

"He says he hates it, but I can tell he's jealous. He never told us anything growing up, but he knows a lot of legends about Oceanids. He seemed to think you bring good luck and is jealous that I will have good luck now, too."

"Does he think what we've been through is good luck?" There had been more pain and heartbreak in the past few months since she had joined the siren than she had all year living in Florida.

Sam shrugged. "It's kind of been good luck since the get go when you really think of it. There were many times that Tim could have killed you; that the other mer could have kidnapped you; that others could have found out about you changing into a siren or about our bond. Yet it never happened. While I fully admit it hasn't been easy, we've had our share of good luck. And that kind of makes me look forward to this war. I have the only Oceanid in existence on my side. I'd say that might just push things in my favor."

Whitney sat up and stretched as there was another crash in the house. She didn't jump this time. It sounded like pots hitting the floor or maybe the wall. There was some cursing that went with it.

"Sorry they had to stay here," Whitney told Sam. He was one for privacy.

He just shrugged. "They're here to help, so I can't complain. At least I bear your Oceanid mark, and they haven't tried to kill me. Yet ..." Sam held up his right arm. Her pink circle was there on his arm, too, but she was sure she had never put a scale on him.

"How?"

"I think the mate bond makes me one automatically. As soon as you changed, I felt it. Then the first time I turned into a siren, I saw my tail had changed. We're together in this; so if you're an Oceanid, then I'm one, too."

Whitney smiled as he reached for her hand to pull her

back to the bed. She resisted, though she would much rather spend all day in bed with him anytime. They still had one more step to go to finish making her Oceanids.

"What do we need to do now?" Sam was already on the same page. He knew she wasn't going to stop until she finished what she needed to do.

"Tell your father to order all the siren into the water, just at the edge should be fine as long as their arm is under the water, and I'll contact the Selkie to do the same," Whitney explained some of it.

Sam nodded as he stood up and pulled board shorts on.

*'Mace?'* Whitney tried reaching out to the Selkie king. If you could have the mark passed from a mate, then he was now an Oceanid, too.

Sam held out his hand, and they began walking down to the nearest shore with the bucket of her scales in his other hand. They had snuck out the back door of his place to avoid the cursing hunter who was still trying to cook.

*'Whitney?'* the Selkie king replied back. *'How the heck are you in my head?'*

*'The same way you are now probably sporting some cool purple marks on your body.'*

*'Shoot. I didn't notice,'* Mace replied.

Whitney could see through his eyes that he had more markings on him than his daughter did. How he couldn't notice was beyond her.

*'Can you get all your Selkie into the water? I want to turn them before the fighting starts so that the hunters on the island don't attack any of you if you make it to shore.'*

*'You're around here somewhere, and I didn't notice you?"*

*'No. I'm still on the island. I plan to dump some into the water, and they should make their way to you. I think—'*

*'You're going to send scales to us where we're hiding?'*

*'I have no idea how, but it'll work. I know it will. Just get in the water.'* She didn't have time to explain it or how she

knew. It was like a deep feeling of what to do without actually being told—like intuition.

Sam stopped at the water's edge. Men, women—old and young—and children were all standing in the water. Sam saw each face turn to them as they drew near and he was beginning to feel what his father felt being king. Every face gazed back with hopeful, trusting eyes. Not a single siren worried or questioned what they were doing. Sam was going to be their leader eventually, and they were already ready to follow him. He was beginning to feel the power of what it meant to be king. It was overwhelming and awe-inspiring at the same time.

"Should I say something?" Whitney whispered to him. She wasn't as comfortable with the stares they were getting. Sam squeezed her hand.

"For those of you gathered here in the lagoon," Sam started; he didn't let go of her hand as he talked, but Whitney was glad he didn't expect her to say anything, "we've been given a great gift by the ocean gods. As it turns out, my mate, Whitney, isn't a siren after all. She's an Oceanid. This alone will bring us luck in the coming battle, but even more than that. Whitney went before the night human council and brought us clemency. We are allowed to go ashore and will no longer be hunted. To be part of the group that's now safe, we need to do one more thing. We need to make you all into Oceanids, too."

Faces around the water were filled with awe and happiness. No one had ever thought they would be allowed on shore. Most of them had grown up on the island, as had their parents before them and their parents before them. Going back to land had never been an option because of the hunters. And now it was. Whitney got the distinct feeling that many of the mer wanted to be able to be on land, but even more so they wanted to exist in a world where they didn't fear their every move. She completely understood that after only living as a siren for months, not years as everyone around her had.

"Would you like to do the honors?" Sam asked, holding the bucket up for Whitney.

"I suppose since I'm the lucky one after all." She winked at him as she accepted the bucket.

Whitney wasn't sure how it was going to work, but she was sure all she had to do was pour her scales into the water. Without any more fanfare, she did just that. At first, they floated on top of the water, leaving a big pink circle, but soon enough they began to swirl and moved under the surface. On their own, they moved away, not following any current pattern or even being pulled by the waves that hit the shore softly. From there she couldn't see them anymore, but she felt them as they moved. One by one, her scales attached to people. Each new person was added to her new mer world, and she felt each one of them. Flashes of memories and feelings hit her each time a new person joined her.

The siren in the waters around the island were all marked, and the scales spread out farther. They found their way to the Selkie and began to mark them. It was amazing to feel each person as they were added into her new clan. As if the scales knew exactly what she wanted, they continued to move and mark people as she knew they would. Once the Selkie were marked, there were still more scales left. There were really going to be enough to do what she wanted. The last of the scales scattered in the water and sought out the good mer lurking around the island among the ones that wanted to kill off the siren. She felt as each new kind of mer was added to her group. As she suspected, there were good mer in each clan. They had more allies than they could have ever imagined.

Without wasting any time, it was time to give them their out. Speaking mentally to her new clan, she gave them the message she had been waiting to share.

*'If you look down and see a pink mark on your right arm, you have been deemed good enough to join the Oceanid*

*race. My name is Whitney, and I've been given the gift of being an Oceanid. On behalf of the mer, I went before the night human council, and they gave a pardon to the siren I protect, and any person I'd given that mark to. With that mark, you are now free to go to land and even collect blood from night human blood banks. As long as you are deemed good by not harming other mer or killing day humans, you'll be free from the hunters. I'm asking any person that wants to join this new mer world to not fight against the siren. This is an island filled with Oceanids, and if you do raise arms against us, you lose your chance at freedom on land forever.'*

That was it. Now it was up to them. She hoped what she said would be enough to sway them as it had the Selkie, and a small part of her knew it would be. The majority of the mer that her scales found would be returning home. She could live with that. Some would stay to fight out of what they thought was honor. She couldn't save everyone, and they all had a choice. It was theirs to make, and it was her job to give them the option their clans weren't offering them. Now it was time to prepare for war, because it was coming. *Soon.*

## CHAPTER 10

**More people arrived** to help. Sam had no clue who all the exotic animals were, but they came with Whitney's witch friend, so he at least knew they were skinwalker night humans. He wasn't a fan of fighting alongside lions, tigers, and bears, but at this point, he couldn't be picky. They'd take any ally they could get. Whitney had explained that they were still human, even if they looked exactly like their animal counterpart to the point he thought maybe he could have seen one or more in the zoo the last time he went as a kid.

"Are you sure Marl is enough to send with the women and children? We could always ask a few younger ones to go with," Sam asked his father, trying to stay on task instead of wondering about all their new visitors.

They had already boarded up the schoolhouse, and that was going to be their safe house for those who weren't involved in the fighting. The mates to all the males had to stay out of the battle because if they did join, then killing one person could kill two. And for the most part, the females didn't want to join the main battle. They were mostly occupied with protecting the young and the old and using the healing water to keep their other half alive.

Marl was one of the oldest siren that had been advising Sam's father for years. He wasn't in the shape to fight, but offered to help the women and children stay safe. The women might have to protect him if it came to it, and Sam didn't agree with his father's choice to not send at least a small group of siren to keep the safe house safe.

"I'll be there with the female greens. We will keep everyone safe," Whitney told Sam.

It had taken him over an hour to convince her that she wasn't going to be a part of the main battle. It was a hard deal to make as Nic, who wasn't fully healed, was going to be fighting. He worked on his argument in his head before going to her with it, and it was still a battle of wills. Whitney just wasn't like normal siren women, and that was the hardest part for Sam.

"Marl isn't the only old-timer going up there. We have Mitchell, Ramon, and Stan. That should be enough to guard both doors," the king replied, not looking up from what he was writing.

The confrontation was only moments away. His father was going to walk down to the shore and release the barrier on the lagoon side of the island, and they were going to face the mer head on. No more waiting. Everything had been planned for, and everyone was ready.

Grasping Whitney's hand, Sam pulled her outside his father's office.

"My mom already took the children and women up to the school. They have a few buckets of healing water, but if they need more, you know where to get it." Sam was in full planning mode. He didn't want anything to go wrong. It wasn't just the siren he was fighting for now; he was fighting for Whitney and her Oceanid world, too.

"Yes. And as soon as I try to persuade the mer to leave, I have to go up there, too. I know. I know. I get it. You need to concentrate." Whitney added the last part a little sourly.

"Thank you." Sam leaned down, pulling her face to his. She needed to know he meant it. Even if it offended her, he did need her safe. There was no way he would be giving it his all fighting if she was there. He would be watching over her. He couldn't help it.

His father came out of his office, interrupting them. He didn't stop as he walked past and made his way down to the beach where everyone was waiting. It didn't matter, either. They had already been over everything. Sam was going to lead the charge as his father was going to use most of his energy to deactivate part of the wall keeping the island safe. It would've been easier to take the whole thing down, but they needed to direct the mer attacking to where they wanted them to come ashore. They weren't prepared to fight all around the island. Therefore, the king was going to rewrite the borders of the barrier to lead them to the beach and the waiting siren.

Sam pulled Whitney with him after his father. As they drew closer to the beach, they began to pass their allies. Whitney's old clan had returned with Cassie, and animals of all shapes and sizes stood around waiting for the battle to begin. Then there was the row of hunters. They were a small bunch, but as Sam had convinced his father, they were worth at least half a dozen siren each in fighting skill. His father knew that much even if he didn't want to admit it. And lastly, they came to the warm sand that was going to be stained with blood by the time the night was through. His fellow siren were all standing around, weapons in hand and ready for battle.

The king took his position on a rock overlooking the battle. It was Whitney's friend Jax's job to keep the king safe where he stood in the open. He was needed to sit there and keep the barrier in place while the fighting went on. Everyone knew that was the job of the king as the barrier was connected to his blood. What they didn't know was the old man wanted to be on the shore beside them fighting. It was killing him to just sit there. Sam could feel his disappointment.

Sam let go of Whitney's hand and left her with the row of hunters. He didn't want her any closer, and he trusted them to keep her safe. Though he was a not a fan of them scraping her scales off, he still knew they would never let harm fall her. Leaning down and placing one last kiss on her head, he turned and headed into the pack of waiting siren.

Nic was already there with his other brothers, and handed

Sam his own weapons. Sam began to strap daggers on his legs and an extra sword on his back. All night humans preferred to fight with old-fashioned weapons, as they felt things such as guns could be hexed. That was actually another advantage of having hunters. They never let their weapons leave their side and thus never had to worry. Jax, hidden in a tree with a rifle, was all they needed to keep his father safe.

"Ready for this?" Nic asked, as he passed over a large, spear-tipped staff to Sam.

"I'm ready, but I would still prefer it if we found something else for Ken to do," Sam replied.

It wasn't that he didn't trust his brother. Ken was a decent fighter, but Sam knew they needed him more for planning than fighting. If it came to a mass change in strategy, Ken had to figure it out and get the king to relay it all to everyone. Ideally, Ken should be staying beside the king in a vantage point to view the fight and make adjustments, but Ken had refused to just sit by their father. He wanted to prove himself as a son of the king, and for that Sam didn't blame him.

*'I am ready whenever you are,'* Sam's father said to him silently.

Sam glanced over at the old man as he stood with his own staff. He was peering out into the sea. With the sun going down, the light was fading, but their vision made it easy to still see. The mer behind the barrier knew something was coming and more were there than the day before.

Taking a deep breath, Sam turned to face the waiting men. "Tonight, we gather here for something that has never come to our island. The mer outside the barrier want us dead. They want war." Sam looked at the men standing around him. "We are ready for this, and we cannot fail. Our families are depending on us to win, and beyond them, we have a second reason to fight our hardest. After tonight, we will be free. You have all met my mate, and she placed her life on the line for us to get freedom within the night human world. Now, all we need is freedom from the mer that wish us dead."

Sam walked down the shore a little and looked into the faces of mer that he had known since he was a child. Most of them were years older than him, but they had always been around as he grew up. They were all now standing beside him, ready to fight. It was very possible that some, if not all, might end up dead. He could be looking at them for the last time, but he couldn't let that stop him.

"We aren't in this alone. We have friends. Behind you are a line of hunters. While they once hunted us, they are now our allies. They will fight beside us. And behind them are the night humans that my mate was part of once—the skinwalkers. They are here to help also as they believe in us and our cause. We have never had allies before, and we have never ventured outside our mer world, but this is the freedom we get when this is done. We won't just be mer; we will be night humans."

Cheers of approval went up around him. Sam couldn't bring himself to smile as many of those men would die in the process of getting that freedom. He knew what war meant, and was ready for it. Most of them had never fought in a battle before, but they were about to now. He didn't want to bring that reality to his island, yet it was there waiting just outside the border.

"We went over this earlier, but don't step in the water. Stay on land and don't let them leave the sand. We keep them from our homes, and we end it here on this beach."

More cheers of approval sounded. They were ready, or as ready as they would ever be.

Sam turned one last time to look at Whitney where she stood, behind the line of siren.

*'I love you,'* he called to her.

Whitney gave him a little smile back. *'Please try to not get too cut up. I don't need any new scars.'*

Sam gave her a grin. Of course, she was worried about number of scars and not over him dying. She was the legendary Oceanid after all. She was all the luck they needed.

*'And I love you, too.'* This time there was no joking. Even Whitney couldn't predict the future.

Sam nodded to her and then turned to his father. War was about to begin, and he was ready.


**Whitney waited to** see the mer come far enough to the beach to need to rise up and walk in their human forms or semi-human forms. She had been expecting a variety as she had met more than one other mer clan, but it was still shocking. The bright yellow hair or deep red signified one clan, but it was the old lady with shriveled skin and waist-length clumpy gray hair that made her shiver. The old lady looked right at her and smiled with rotting yellow teeth showing.

"I command any mer that holds my mark to freeze. You were given the chance to leave and chose not to; now you will watch as the world fights around you. I command any advancing mer to also stop," Whitney said both verbally and mentally at the same time with her siren command.

Most of the mer just kept moving. They figured they must have done something to their hearing to be immune to the siren song, even if the king didn't think it was possible. Two of the mer on the left side of the shore, close enough that more than half their body was visible above the water, stopped in their tracks. Mer behind them just kept coming and didn't stop to see what they were doing. Two was more than nothing, but Whitney had hoped to stop a few more than that. More than three or four dozen were coming ashore as she watched, including the creepy old lady.

"You have to leave now," Jade said, pulling Whitney out of her disappointment.

Whitney nodded to her.

"Stay safe," she told her friend. She felt guilty running off, but she had made a promise to Sam, and the people in the school were close to defenseless. She wanted to be in the main fight, but they needed her more.

"You, too," Jade added, not turning from the shore and watching the fight already beginning. Beside her, her mother smiled, like she couldn't wait to join them.

Whitney pushed past the hunters and then the skinwalkers. She didn't want to look too closely at who had come with Cassie. Odds were good that she knew most of the people who'd come to help, but thankfully in their animal forms, she couldn't be too certain.

"Uncle John didn't let him come, even though he begged," Cassie said, stepping beside her and walking the path up the hill to the school with Whitney. Cassie wasn't to join the main fight either.

"Who?" Okay, Whitney knew who, but she wanted to be sure.

"Your brother. He's been getting stronger every moon, but he still has a long way to go. John ordered him to stay behind."

Whitney nodded. She didn't want her younger brother in the siren battle and was relieved he'd been left home. He had almost been killed once alongside her over a year ago. This way he was safe. She knew he was probably angry, but John was able to handle anyone. Who in their right mind would defy a man who turned into a bear on the full moon, and was close to being one the rest of the time?

It didn't take long to make it up to the school. Whitney looked inside and found the women sitting and waiting with the children. Sam's mother was moving between women as cuts would appear on them. As Sam had said, she had a bucket of water with her that she was quickly applying to each person. She worked efficiently and didn't need the help of the women assisting her. At the front and back doorways, the old men sat with their own swords at the ready as if they were prepared to battle. It was strange to see the old men ready for battle in leather vests that matched what lots of the siren wore for protection from claws of the other various mer. They probably and hopefully wouldn't see that kind of action. Marl appeared uncomfortable in his with long sleeves underneath.

Whitney nodded to him before leaving the women and children alone. The windows had been all boarded up, so from the outside, you only knew there was someone in there if you saw one of the open doorways. Whitney peered into the surrounding woods and could see each of her green siren Oceanids walking around, keeping their distance and remaining hidden while protecting the village.

"I need a better view of the beach," Whitney said to Cassie, who stood just behind her.

Walking around to the side ladder that most of the buildings on the island had, Whitney began to climb up to the roof of the schoolhouse. Cassie followed, and somehow her panther was right behind her. Who knew that large cats could climb ladders?

From the top of the schoolhouse, Whitney had a better view of the beach. More mer were coming out of the water, and more siren were attacking. It was a never-ending cycle that was ending up with piles of bodies on the beautiful white sand. Whitney looked down as a cut appeared on her arm. Cassie handed her a cloth.

"I told him not to get all cut up. I don't need more scars than I already have," Whitney complained, and Cassie smiled. Joking was the only way Whitney could deal with the fact that Sam was getting hurt.

Whitney tried to find Sam in the mass of people on the beach, all swinging weapons around, but it was impossible in the fading light. What wasn't impossible was seeing the king sitting on his stone above the fight, his expression laced with complete determination. Every now and then a mer would get the idea to attack him and start to climb up the stone. Each time, they would fall back to the ground, unmoving. Jax was an expert shot and kept the whole thing working. Without the king, there would be much more chaos and a very good chance the siren wouldn't win. Whitney was starting to believe maybe she had a little Oceanid luck in making friends with hunters like Jax.

Cassie stood up as the panther's ears perked.

"There's someone close," Cassie whispered to Whitney.

Whitney shot down the ladder with Cassie right behind her. Neither one made a sound on their descents.

'Where?' Whitney mouthed to her friend.

Either Cassie or the panther had better hearing than her and she didn't care which it was. If someone was close, she would rather take care of it than let one of her greens come upon the person. Whitney was by far better trained in hand-to-hand combat. Cassie pointed into the trees and toward a different path than the one they had taken to the school from beach. Someone was trying to sneak their way to the school house. Whitney hurried that way as quietly as she could. As least she was still as silent as her old night human form had been.

When they got close enough, Whitney could hear the same fighting that Cassie and her cat must have heard. There was someone close, but they were fighting with someone else already. Whitney dove off the path and into the trees to help out whatever green had come upon the intruder, and was surprised to find Sam's older brother and traitor, Tim, with a rope wrapped around Jade's neck. She was gasping for air, but that didn't stop her as she jabbed behind her with a knife in her hand. Tim was hit several times, but still didn't let go. Whitney stood and watched, unsure how to enter the fight without getting cut by Jade in the process. She wasn't going down easily.

Suddenly the ground around them began to frost over, and it crept up Tim's legs. Before anyone knew what was going on, Tim was frozen in his position. Whitney didn't question where it came from and ran over to her friend, removing the rope from around her neck. Jade fell to her feet, gasping for air.

"I was in the middle of everything when I saw him slip by," Jade finally explained once she caught her breath. "I followed him up here, and once I knew where we were going, I jumped in to stop him. Your boyfriend's dick of an older brother wanted to go kill innocent children and women. How much less of a man could he be?"

Jade was standing up, yet still, quite a bit winded. She was fighting for her life, but more than that, she was fighting for the lives of everyone in the schoolhouse.

Whitney turned to Tim and stared at him. Even for him, that was low. He hated the siren and wanted them dead, but the hate was more for his family. That was what didn't click for Whitney. He didn't want all the siren dead, because if they were, he could never be king over them. It made no sense to kill them all off.

"You're going to let me into your mind and let me see what the plans are from the attacking mer," Whitney told him with force in her voice.

"You are weaker than my brother ... good luck, little girl. I was thinking of keeping you around once we win since you're easy on the eyes, but I've changed my mind. It'll be much more fun to kill you in front of my brother and see him suffer as he dies, too." Tim glared at her.

Whitney didn't hear his words very clearly. She was already going into his mind. Whitney had only been completely in Sam's mind before; it felt really odd to be in someone else's mind. Sam's mind was filled with love and honor—the two most important things for him—but Tim's was like walking through sludge. His head was filled with evil thoughts. People he wanted to kill and how he wanted to kill them. And then there were all the ways he planned to get more power. That seemed to be all he thought about, wanting to kill people and get power. She didn't want to stay long in the poison that was Tim's mind.

"Show me what your plans are," Whitney ordered, not leaving his mind.

"No," Tim replied, and then there were images in front of Whitney. It was exactly what she needed to see. "Impossible. You can't order me around," he protested, realizing what she was finally doing.

Tim continued to complain, but Whitney focused on the images of their battle plans. The mer seemed to understand that a small opening wasn't to their advantage. At the rate they were going, the siren stood a chance. They needed the barrier from the whole island down. Tim had offered to go kill the queen, and thus the king, in order to do so. There were more mer waiting on the other side of the island, ready for the barrier to be released.

Whitney pulled out of his mind.

"You really want your father dead?" she asked Tim as he stared sullenly at her. He did not like the fact that she had been in his mind, but he seemed to like the fact that she was stronger than him even less.

"The old man chose Sam—Sam, of all people—and it turns out he was always going to choose him. I never stood a chance. So yes, I want the old man dead. That's not news."

*'Mace, the other mer are on the opposite side of the island,'* Whitney told their ally as she stared at Tim.

She wasn't going to let him win with his complaining to get into an argument. She wasn't going to stoop to arguing with him. He didn't deserve to win. He deserved to rot for all the bad he had done over the years. She had seen inside his head, and he didn't just think evil thoughts, he acted out a lot of them as well. Pulling into his pace was not going to work.

"Well, too bad we have you now, and your plan won't work. The siren are going to win this one," Whitney told him, before turning from him to walk away.

"Who said I was the only one sent to kill the queen?" Tim

could barely move, but he managed a small smile.

Whitney thought back for a minute. Tim was the only one that had gotten close to the schoolhouse. She was sure if there were more people coming, Cassie or her jaguar would have heard them. She glanced over to her friend, who seemed to read her mind and shook her head in reply. There was no one else around. The people protecting the women were all her Oceanids. She had changed each of the greens personally. But she hadn't changed the men or the women in the schoolhouse one by one. Any one of them could be a traitor. She hadn't thought to check and make sure they were all her Oceanids now.

"I'll take care of him," Jade said as she understood that Whitney needed to run back, but couldn't leave Tim.

"The ice will last for at least another ten minutes," Cassie explained. "Just have him tied up before then."

Jade nodded to Cassie as Whitney took off back to the school, the whole time searching her mind as she thought of the people left behind. How could she have missed someone not being changed? She didn't like to link to their minds, and now she was linked to over a thousand. She should have checked each person left behind. The queen was the last weak link in their plan. If someone took her out, the barrier would fall.

**Whitney made it** back to the schoolhouse at the same time she remembered one fact. If someone was running around without a mark, she wouldn't be the only one to notice. Others would notice, too. They had to be hiding it, and then it made sense. The king's old friend Marl was wearing a long-sleeved shirt and seemed uncomfortable in it. The siren weren't shy and never wanted to be covered up. Most of them walked around in what was close to being just a swimsuit all the time. The only reason to cover up would be to hide something.

Whitney burst in the door, making the men sitting there draw their weapons until they realized it was her. Across the room, Marl was standing by the queen. He held a bloody knife in his hand. Whitney ran across the room as the people around began to realize the queen was now slumped over. Without a second thought, Whitney had the knife from his hand, and with one good hit, he was knocked unconscious.

"Mira," Whitney said as she knelt beside the older woman that was their only chance to keep the barrier up now.

Whitney reached for the bucket of healing water and thankfully found there was still some left. Whitney's water manipulation skills were not good, especially when she was stressed, so she just dipped her hand in and scooped out water on the bleeding wound. She pulled back the queen's shirt and found the wound wasn't healing even with the water.

*'Sam, Marl just stabbed your mother,'* Whitney yelled at him across the bond. *'I tried the water, but it didn't work. Why didn't it work?'*

Sam didn't reply, but he was moving across the sand quickly to his father. If the queen was down, soon the king would fall.

*'There's only one thing that the water doesn't heal,'* Sam finally replied as he was beside his father. *'Poison.'* Sam was now dealing with his father slowly losing control of the barrier.

Picking up the blade from the floor, Whitney looked to her friend in the doorway. Cassie hurried over.

"It's poisoned. Would you be able to save her?" Whitney asked hopefully. Cassie was the strongest witch she knew.

"If I had time, but it doesn't look like we do." Cassie pointed down to the queen. She was gasping for breath. It was a fast-acting poison.

"If she falls, then so does the island. We need to get the children out of here and to the secret shore," Whitney said as she stood above the dying queen. She wanted to help her, but there was nothing she could do for poison, especially if Cassie couldn't fix it. They would to evacuate the children and women off the island. This was the last case plan, but she would do it. Everything in her power was going to be needed to save the last of the siren.

"Just let me go get someone. I think he can do it. He's saved other people who were poisoned before. Please let him try, and if it doesn't work, I'll take the children and unbonded siren to shore." Cassie didn't wait for a reply and ran to the nearest tree. Her black cat stayed behind and lay down next to the dying queen.

"Is he safe?" one of the ladies nearby asked in a loud whisper, like she didn't want to anger the cat.

Whitney glanced down at Jared as he kept his head pressed to the side of the queen, her hand resting on his fur.

"He used to be human once until someone killed that part of him with magic. This is all he has left, but he isn't a wild animal," Whitney explained. The cat looked up at her, ready to disagree, but Cassie was already running back into the room.

"She's right here with Jared," Cassie said to the man behind her.

There was a beautiful man with her, but as he neared Whitney saw he wasn't much older than they were. His bright blond hair and blue eyes could match her own. But that wasn't what stood out. It was the slight glow around his skin. It made him more attractive than he must have been as just a human. And the power that followed him ... Whitney still was new to feeling out night humans in her mer skin, but she felt him the moment he set foot on the island. This man was more than special. He didn't look to Whitney as he knelt by the queen.

"It's been maybe three to five minutes maximum," Cassie continued as the man knelt beside the queen on the opposite side from the cat. The panther didn't look up as he stood guard, comforting the dying queen.

"Her name?" The man finally turned his blue eyes to Whitney. She was caught in how they sparkled, and how otherworldly it was. "Whitney, her name?" he asked again, and it was him saying her own name that pulled her out of her trance.

"Mira. She's the mate to the king of the siren. He's holding back a barrier to force the mer come in at only one point, so they targeted her to kill him." Whitney had no idea why she was explaining more than he needed.

"Okay, Mira, this is going to feel funny, but it'll be over before you know it," the man said, placing his hand over the wound.

*'What's going on?'* Sam asked, finally reconnecting. He was busy trying to give power to his father to keep the barrier up.

*'Cassie brought someone to save your mom. He says he can do it,'* Whitney replied as she watched the man's hand glow more than his skin already glowed.

Slowly, he began to pull his hand back, and with it, something came straight out of the wound. He pulled a little bit more before he stopped, a ball hovering above his hand. Whitney had no idea what to say. Heck, she had no idea who the guy was, but it seemed like he just willed the poison out of the queen with only his mind or something. Powerful wasn't even the right word to describe him. He was so much more than that.

The man stood up and held out the hand that wasn't holding the poison to Whitney; his right hand in the gesture to shake her hand.

"Sorry about coming in so rudely. I'm Devin Alexander," he introduced himself like he was just another person, but Whitney knew better. This was Devin. *The* Devin. The Sidhe King. Cassie had gone straight to the legendary Sidhe King to get help. Devin smiled at her, making a dimple appear in his right cheek. If Whitney didn't know who he was, she might have been tempted to hit on him, even though she had a mate and all. He was drop-dead gorgeous and completely off-limits.

"Here," Cassie said as she handed Devin a vial.

Who knew where she got that from? Whitney had a feeling it had been full, and she had just emptied it because that was the only thing that made sense.

"Thanks," Devin replied as he took it and pushed the poison into it. "Do you mind if I take this home to study?" he asked Whitney. She shook her head. "Thanks. I have to get back, but I'd like to do one more thing for you."

Whitney just nodded. She had no idea what more he could do. He had saved the queen and the whole plan for equal footing in the fight. She owed him for that.

Devin walked outside and took a deep breath, as if he was more comfortable outside the building than inside. Walking over to a tree, he placed his hand on it like Cassie did when she traveled through the trees. But instead of leaving, he stood there with his eyes closed and concentrating. After a few moments, he pulled back and smiled again at Whitney.

"That's my thank you for giving your blood to Arianna. She's trying to unite all night humans, and the more she can combine, the better the results will be. You've helped her on her goal, and I owed you for that."

Whitney stared at him. She had no clue what he was talking about. Devin just laughed.

"I am one of her keepers. I know everything that goes on with her even if I'm not there," he explained.

Well, at least that part made more sense, but she had a feeling there was more to the story than that.

Devin reached down to her shin and touched the blood on her leg from yet another cut Sam had taken that she didn't notice. He brushed it onto the tree, and it melted away.

"If you ever need to get ahold of me, just touch your blood to any living plant, and I'll come to you," he explained, placing his hand on the tree again.

"Wait," Whitney finally said before he could disappear. "What the heck did you do, and why are you helping me?"

Devin grinned at her. "Once you talk to your mate you will find all the mer that were fighting you are now tangled in plants, even the ones in the water. That's my thank you to you from Arianna. And as to why? Well, not just because you're Cassie's best friend, but because you and I are legends. We legends have to stick together you know. There aren't many of us around." Devin winked and then was gone.

*'Whitney, everything is done,'* Sam said across the bond. *'Somehow all the mer are tangled up in plants here on land and in the water. It's going to take some time to collect them all, but it's over.'*

Just like Devin had said.

Whitney turned to her friend who was standing in the doorway to the schoolhouse.

"I told you he was strange and unpredictable," Cassie said, like that explained it all.

"And hot. You told me hot, but I didn't know how hot," Whitney teased, and they both laughed.

Just like that, the battle was won. Whitney's choice to go before the night human council had saved everything. The siren, or rather Oceanids, were pardoned. The sirens were safe in the night human world. And in a second moment, Devin stopped the whole fight, and it was done, too. Her world had started over when she joined the night human world for a second time, but she was grateful. Sam had brought her back to where she was meant to be. For that, she was willing to play her part of being a legend. And maybe they could just go back to having a boring life once everything was cleaned up, or maybe not. Whitney understood that what came next would depend on what fate had in store for her, and she was ready for the ride.

# EPILOGUE

**Whitney looked at** her new home. It was larger and closer to their neighbors, but she liked it. It was situated not too far from the shore this time. It was better to be part of the siren island rather than watching over it like Sam's old place had been, and maybe being on a new island also helped. It made things feel safer and a lot more peaceful than walking around a place where many had died, and more had bled.

In the wake of the attack, they were left with hundreds of enemy mer they didn't know what to do with. If they let them go free, they would just group up and attack again. If they killed them off, they would be no better off than they had been to begin with. Luckily, the siren found a solution they all could live with.

The old siren island became a prison for the mer who had attacked the siren. They weren't allowed on the mainland because the hunters were still allowed to kill them, and they weren't allowed to go free. Cassie was able to set up a spell that would hold them there forever. Only about one-hundred yards out to sea was a barrier that went from the ocean bottom into the sky that no man or object other than the fish and other mammals in the sea could pass. And really, how much of a punishment was it to be stuck on a tropical island for the rest of your life?

The siren then moved to their second island. While Tim had been staying there, he didn't do anything bad to the place. He kept up the original barrier to keep it protected. It didn't take much work to move everyone there. And the best part was that it was closer to the mainland. Going back and forth took no time at all.

"We're going to be late," Trudy complained to Whitney

as she looked back at the water.

The water still called to her, but it was a happy sound that seemed to say, "Come back when you have time." There were no more urges to walk toward it like there had first been and no more urges to drain people dry either. Everyone had full access to the night human blood banks, and all the Oceanids were well-fed instead of on the brink of starving. Life had taken a complete one-eighty, all due to one choice to stand before the night human council and ask for forgiveness.

"You know your aunt is going to be mad if we're late," Trudy tried again to get Whitney to move from her spot.

Okay, that much was true. Whitney stood up and transformed into her legs, being sure to scoop up her clothes as she did so she wouldn't get them wet. Running after her friend up the sandy beach, it didn't take much to climb the path back to the parking lot behind the diner. Sam was already in his car with the engine running.

"We're going to be late," he told her.

Leaning over, Whitney gave him a peck on his cheek.

"Come on, lovebirds, keep that to a minimum," Tina complained next to Trudy from the back seat. "Some of us without mates don't want to lose our breakfast before we get there."

"Tell me about it. I'm nervous enough that I am going to trip and make a fool of myself," Trudy replied.

Sam peeled out of the parking lot and onto the street faster than necessary. At that rate, they weren't going to be late, and they'd make it on time to the school. There was nothing to worry about. No one was going to be late or trip as they walked. They were Oceanids, after all, and way too graceful to trip, even in their black billowy gowns.

Whitney smiled as her friends helped each other attach their square black hats while the car zoomed toward school. It was graduation day, a day she never imagined would come. She hadn't thought too much about her future, but once she had been changed into an outlawed mer, Whitney figured it was a life on the island or a life on the run. Now she got to have a life of her own choosing. She was allowed to go on land any time she wanted. She could go to college, get a real job—all that stuff people dreamt of. Life was turning out to be better than she ever could have guessed it would be. Maybe, just maybe, she had a bit of Oceanid luck after all, and being a legend wouldn't be so bad.

# ACKNOWLEDGEMENTS

**To you**, the reader. <u>Thank You</u> for taking the time to read this story. If you liked it, please leave a review on your favorite online bookseller (or all of them!) and connect with me social media. The greatest help you can do to keep a writer going is to support them by spreading the word about their books.

Also I would like to thank my editors and cover designers. A good editor is essential to getting the story correct (and in my case- several). Thank you so much, Kathie at Kat's Eye Editing, Melissa at There for You Editing, and Ashton Brammer. They work so hard to get you guys the best book. A thank-you to my *AMAZING* cover artist Jessica for such a pretty cover- doesn't she do great work!! I'm beyond fortunate to have found these wonderful professionals to work with.

I'd also like to thank my hubby – who is the only reason I actually even published. He gives me time when I need it to work on my stories. He encourages me to keep going each and every day on this adventure. And he does all the behind-the-scenes effort to make this work. This would be so much harder without his help. So thank you, B. for pushing me off the deep end (or the cliff as I see it sometimes). And a great big thanks to my little munchkins who keep me going from before the sun comes up 'til long after it sets. Love you AK, KB, and EM.

*<u>Thank you so much for taking the time to read my novel!!</u>*

## ABOUT B. KRISTIN McMICHAEL

Originally from Wisconsin, B. Kristin currently resides in Ohio with her husband, three small children, and three cats. A former cell biologist, she now does the mom thing of chasing kids, baking cookies, and playing outside while writing full time. She is a fan of all YA/NA fantasy and science fiction. Find her at www.bkristinmcmichael.com and Twitter, Facebook, Instagram, and Goodreads under B. Kristin McMichael.

# BOOKS BY B KRISTIN MCMICHAEL

- To Stand Beside Her

**<u>Chalcedony Chronicles</u>**
- Carnelian
- Chrysoprase
- Aventurine
- Chrysocolla

## *<u>The Night Human World series:</u>*

*The Blue Eyes Trilogy (series 1)*
- The Legend of the Blue Eyes
- Becoming a Legend
- Winning the Legend

*The Day Human Trilogy (series 2)*
- The Day Human Prince
- The Day Human King
- The Day Human Way

*The Skinwalkers Witchling Trilogy (series 3)*
- The Witchling's Apprentice
- The Wendigo Witchling
- The Witchling Seer

*The Merworld Trilogy (series 4)*
- Water and Blood
- Songs and Fins
- Scales and Legends

*The Hunter Trilogy (series 5)*
- The Night Human Hunter
- The Night Human Heir

Made in the USA
Middletown, DE
26 January 2018